M
Hamish Macbeth series, as well as numerous Regency romances. Her Agatha Raisin books have been turned into a TV series on Sky One. She lives in Paris and in a Cotswolds village that is very much like Agatha's beloved Carsely.

M.C. Beaton

Agatha Raisin AND the
DEAD RINGER

CONSTABLE

CONSTABLE

First published in the US in 2018 by Minotaur Books,
an imprint of St Martin's Press

First published in Great Britain in 2018 by Constable

This paperback edition published in Great Britain in 2019 by Constable

A CIP catalogue record for this book
is available from the British Library.

ISBN 978-1-47212-697-9

Typeset in Palatino by Photoprint, Torquay
Printed and bound in Great Britain by
CPI Group (UK) Ltd, Croydon CR0 4YY

Papers used by Constable are from well-managed forests and other
responsible sources

Constable
An imprint of
Little, Brown Book Group
Carmelite House
50 Victoria Embankment
London EC4Y 0DZ

An Hachette UK Company
www.hachette.co.uk

www.littlebrown.co.uk

This book is dedicated to my five pillars of wisdom:
Hope Dellon
Hannah O'Grady
Barbara Lowenstein
Mary South
Krystyna Green

Chapter One

The Cotswolds in the West Midlands are rated as a beauty spot. They are reckoned to be the only beauty spot made by man, the attraction lying in their gardens and thatched cottages. Busloads of tourists are taken to Stow-on-the-Wold, the Slaughters and places like Bourton-on-the-Water to look at other tourists scrambling for places in tea shops, not realising that there are a great number of pretty villages off the beaten track.

Such was the village of Thirk Magna. The residents were proud of the fact that few tourists ever sullied the quiet of their rural village, even though the pride of the village, the Norman church of St Ethelred, boasted one of the finest sets of bells in the country.

And there were no bell ringers more dedicated than Mavis and Millicent Dupin. They were identical twins in their early forties. They dressed alike in twinsets: baggy tweed skirts and brogues. Both had long, thin faces and long, thin noses. They were very proud of the Dupin nose which they claimed had come over with William the Conqueror. The twins lived in the manor house, a square Georgian building overlooking the duck pond.

Their normally placid lives had been thrown into turmoil, for the bishop was to visit and a special peal of bells was to be rung for him.

The twins summoned the other six bell ringers to their home to decide on a special peal.

The six were normally united in their dislike of the twins and their passionate love of campanology, although some had joined the troupe for other reasons and subsequently found out that they had developed a love of bell ringing. They shuffled into the drawing room of the manor house and waited while Mavis wheeled in a trolley laden with tea and cakes and her sister, Millicent, began to hand round napkins. Helen Toms, the vicar's wife, hated those napkins, for they were double damask and embroidered in one corner with the twins' initials. Somehow, Helen always managed to spill a little tea on one of those precious napkins and Millicent would snatch it from her, making distressed clucking sounds, like a hen about to lay. Helen, with her wings of dark hair and her clear complexion, would have been attractive had she not been so edgy and nervous.

Because of inverted snobbery, Harry Bury, the sexton, considered himself a man of the people and the sisters, with their private income, parasites. He had a red face with a perpetual smile and small beady eyes filled with distrust. Julian Brody was a handsome lawyer, two times divorced, though no one quite knew why because he was a relative newcomer to the village. The twins made a great fuss of him to the irritation of Colin Docherty, a teacher of physics at a nearby high school, who had previously been the favourite. He had a nervous habit of cracking his knuckles and whistling through a gap in his front teeth. Joseph Merrydown, the butcher, was so red in the face, like a rare sirloin, that the others often feared he might have a stroke during practice.

Helen Toms was always surprised that the men did not chase after Gloria Buxton, a curvaceous blonde with a salon tan and collagen-enhanced lips. Gloria had been divorced from her banker husband for ten years, and, from her blonde hair to her stilettos, seemed an odd person to take up bell ringing. But as Helen's friend Margaret Bloxby, who was married to a vicar as well, had said, bell ringing was not a hobby, it was an obsession.

Mavis rapped her spoon against her cup as a sign that the meeting was to begin and, not to be outdone, Millicent rapped her spoon as well.

In her high fluting voice, Millicent got in first. 'It is a great honour, this forthcoming visit by the bishop. In his honour, it would be a good idea if we could aim for the longest bell ringing, the Oxford Treble Bob Major.'

Joseph Merrydown gasped. 'But that took over ten hours, that did. T'would kill us, that would.'

Julian Brody googled the achievement on his phone. 'Hey! That was seventeen thousand, eight hundred and twenty-four changes.'

Bell ringing is like no other type of music. It is not written on a standard score. Bells start ringing down the scale, 1 2 3 4 5. But to ring changes, bells change their order each time they strike and it is all done from memory.

The butcher and the sexton were bell ringers like their parents before them, the lawyer because it amused him, the teacher because he was lonely and the vicar's wife because her husband had insisted she do it. The divorcée because it was great exercise and she had her eye on the lawyer.

The twins held sway over the others because their father had spent his own money refurbishing the bells and had claimed the bells as his property and had left them to his twin daughters.

A clamour of protests from the others fell on the twins' deaf ears. They were as part of the church as the damp hassocks, the faulty heating and, of course, the bells.

That was until Gloria Buxton said, 'I can't see the bishop waiting all those hours. He will stay for only a short time and bugger off.'

'He will learn of its importance,' said Millicent passionately. 'It will be the talk of the country.'

Julian had assiduously been doing research on his phone. 'That's the bishop of Mircester you're talking about? The Right Reverend Peter Salver-Hinkley?'

'Yes, why?' demanded Millicent.

'I've got a picture here of him sleeping his way through Grandsire Trebles by the bell ringers of Duxton-in-the-Hedges. Surely a short welcoming peal, dear ladies, and then you will have time to talk to him. If you persist in this long ring marathon, he will be long gone before you can say hello.'

With that odd telepathy of theirs, the sisters looked at each other and then left the room.

'They in love with 'im, or what?' asked the butcher.

'I think it could be called a sort of schoolgirl crush,' said Julian.

'At their age?' said the sexton.

'They're in their forties and still got all their hormones.' Julian gave a catlike smile. 'At the moment, they are wrestling with their passion for bell ringing with their passion for the bishop.'

'Must be mad,' said Gloria Buxton. 'I mean, all those Anglican preachers have dead white faces, thick lips and rimless glasses.'

To break the following embarrassed silence – for the local vicar, Helen Toms' husband, looked exactly like that – Julian said, 'Not this bishop. He's sex on legs.'

'Cripes and be damned,' said the butcher, Joseph Merrydown.

'Here, take a gander at his pic,' said Julian, holding out his phone. 'Beautiful, isn't he? Like one of those old-fashioned illustrations in children's books of one of King Arthur's knights.'

The bishop had a white, alabaster face, thin and autocratic with a high-bridged nose and a thin, humorous mouth. His hair was a mass of thick, black, glossy curls. His eyelids were curved, giving his face the odd look of a classical statue.

'His mother, it says here,' said the sexton, breathing heavily through his nose, 'was Lady Fathering, eldest daughter of the Earl of Hadshire. She adopted 'im. Well, that explains it, I means ter say, why he looks so grand.'

'You old snob,' drawled Gloria. 'Did you expect him

5

to be as droopy as the usual bish? Or would you like him to be African?'

'I'll report you to the Race Relations board,' snarled the sexton, and that was followed by a heavy silence while everyone reflected that freedom of speech had left the British Isles, sometimes to a ridiculous extent.

Colin Docherty, the schoolteacher, broke the silence. 'I think you've put the right idea in their heads. It'll be the sherry and nibbles welcome.'

'I'll do that,' said Helen Toms.

'I'd better do it,' said Gloria. 'The bishop's taste is surely a bit above a village's 1950s idea of refreshment.'

Helen Toms blushed miserably.

'You mean she can't serve up soggy vol-au-vents like yours?' jeered the teacher.

'I do not serve soggy vol-au-vent,' howled Gloria.

The door to the drawing room opened and the twins came back in. 'We have decided a welcome reception after a short peal is all that is necessary. The reception will be held in our drawing room.'

'I think it should be held in the vicarage drawing room,' protested Julian.

'May I point out that the manor house drawing room is the grander of the two?'

'The vicarage one is more welcoming than this Victorian mausoleum,' said Julian. 'I mean, rickety bamboo tables full of old photos. Glass cases of stuffed birds. Let's put it to a vote. Raise hands for the vicarage.'

All except the twins and Gloria voted for the vicarage. 'Look at it this way, girls,' said Julian in a conciliatory tone of voice, 'the church and the vicar are what he wants to see.'

Julian walked Helen back to the vicarage. 'Don't look so worried,' he said. 'I've got a friend coming to stay. He's a chef in a Paris restaurant. I'll get him to do the nibbles.'

'But I'm on a budget.'

'My contribution. Don't protest. Just dying to put several noses out of joint.'

'You might put Peregrine's nose out of joint. He expected any reception to be in the village hall.'

'I'd better talk to him. He'll bully you out of it. You know he's mean.'

'You must not criticise my husband!' yelled Helen.

He looked at her sorrowfully. 'When you're all riled up and full of animation, I could kiss you.'

'Leave me alone!' Helen strode off. But then she stopped. It would be really marvellous to use this chef and surprise everyone. She turned back. 'Julian!'

'Yes, my love?'

'Sorry I was so abrupt. Thank you for the offer. Most grateful.'

When she walked up the vicarage path, her husband was waiting at the door. He had been a great admirer of a former archbishop of Canterbury, Rowan Williams, who had a long white beard, and he was trying to copy his appearance by growing one himself. But it had sprouted in tufts, and, although the hair on his head was white, the beard had grown in ginger.

'What were you shouting about?' he demanded.

'Well, by popular vote, our drawing room is to be used to receive the bishop. A French chef friend of Julian's wants to supply all the welcoming food for free. I told him to forget it.'

Helen was used to manipulating her husband. 'You should have consulted me first,' complained Peregrine in his high fluting voice. 'Do phone Julian and tell him to go ahead.'

With unusual courage, Helen snapped, 'Phone him yourself,' and, pushing past him, went into the house.

The one phone was inconveniently placed on a hall table. Helen heard him dial and then heard him apologise for his wife's 'menopausal' behaviour. She groaned and, twisting round on the sofa, put the cushions over her ears. 'I'm only thirty-eight-years old,' she muttered.

Her husband came in so she sat up. 'Do you know Mrs Bloxby over at Carsely?'

'I have met her on a few occasions,' Helen said.

'I want you to get over there and invite Mrs Bloxby and her husband to the reception. Alf Bloxby was at Cambridge at the same time as the bishop.'

Helen knew Margaret Bloxby to be both quiet and kind. Glad of a chance to escape, she nodded and went out to her old Ford parked outside on the road, the one space in front of the vicarage being reserved for Peregrine's

Daimler. As it was not exactly vintage and no one wanted large gas guzzlers these days, he had bought it very cheaply.

Getting into her car, Helen headed off for Carsely.

Mrs Bloxby looked amused when she received the invitation. 'Of course I'll come, Helen,' she said. 'My husband tells me our bishop was rated a lady killer at Cambridge.'

'But he is not married?'

'He is reported to say he could never meet a lady who could match his beauty. Joking, of course, although he is reported to be quite beautiful.'

The phone rang. 'Could you answer that, dear?' came the voice of Mrs Bloxby's husband from the study.

Mrs Bloxby sighed and picked up the phone. 'It's for you, Helen,' she said. 'Your husband.'

'What does he want now?' said Helen crossly, but she picked up the receiver and said meekly, 'Yes, dear, what is it? Yes, I will try.'

She sighed as she put down the receiver. 'What a demanding bishop! Now, he wants the sleuth of the Cotswolds, Agatha Raisin.'

'Mrs Raisin is a great friend of mine,' said Mrs Bloxby. The doorbell rang. 'In fact, that might even be her. She doesn't work on Saturdays.'

Mrs Bloxby answered the door and came back into the drawing room with a sophisticated-looking woman.

Agatha Raisin had never become countrified. From her Armani suit to her high heels, she looked more suited to Bond Street than a village vicarage.

After the introductions had been made, Helen said timidly, 'Would you ask her, Sarah?'

'Sarah!' exclaimed Agatha. 'Her name is Margaret, although I call her by her surname, a hangover from the now-defunct Ladies Society.'

'I was christened Sarah-Margaret,' said Mrs Bloxby. 'Very confusing. I answer to both. Well, Mrs Raisin, the bishop is visiting Thirk Magna and the right rev is anxious to meet you.'

'Why?' demanded Agatha. 'I will probably be too busy.'

Mrs Bloxby smiled. 'I haven't told you when this party is. Yes, it is a vicarage party, and yes, you need not go because you won't be able to get near him for fawning women.'

Agatha's small bear-like eyes focused on her friend. 'When is this party?'

'Two weeks today,' said Helen. 'At six in the evening.'

Mrs Bloxby handed round sherry and, out of the corner of her eyes, watched the busy wheels of Agatha's brain churning around. 'What's Mrs Bish like?' Agatha asked.

'Isn't one,' said Mrs Bloxby.

'And why do women fawn over him? Oh, I know. He's gay. Churchy women have a weakness for gay men. They can dream without ever having to face the sweaty reality. Just think of all the married women in this country who would rather read a book at bedtime than have to put up with him rolling over on top of them. Oh, the tyranny of the double bed. Hey! I'm sorry. I will go to the ball.' For Agatha had just noticed one large tear rolling down Helen's cheek. 'Helen, why don't you phone your husband and say I have invited you to the pub for lunch?'

'He will demand that I return immediately to cook his lunch.'

'Give it a try.'

Helen dialled home and explained in a quavery voice that Agatha had invited her to lunch. 'Then go, for Heaven's sake,' snarled her husband. 'Just get her to that reception.'

'I can go,' said Helen after she had rung off.

'Right, pub it is. Anyone got a pic of this bishop?'

Helen opened a large handbag like a saddlebag and extracted a parish magazine. 'There he is, Agatha. Front page.'

'I say. You do yourself proud. Glossy and full colour.'

'We have a village geek.'

Agatha looked at a photo of the bishop. He was laughing at something. Now, Agatha had gone to a tough school in a slum area and so she had learned to keep her dreams of knights in armour to herself. Who was it the Lady of Shalott fell for? That one who sang 'Tirra lirra' by the river? Sir Lancelot, surely. How she used to dream that one day he would ride into assembly and scoop her up onto his milk-white steed.

Oh, dear. What have I done? fretted Mrs Bloxby, who had seen bad endings to Agatha's previous obsessions.

11

'Will you be joining us, Margaret?' asked Helen.

'No, I've got a parishioner coming round for advice in half an hour. You know how it is, Helen. Our time is never our own.'

'Leave a note on the door, saying, "Screw you, you pathetic old bag. Either join us in the pub or go home,"' said Agatha.

'Mrs Raisin! Off you go and stop trying to terrify Mrs Toms.'

'I am sorry,' said Agatha, as they walked to the village pub. 'Does your husband bully you?'

'I will not discuss my husband,' said Helen in a thin voice. 'In fact, thank you for your kind invitation but I must get home.' With that, she turned on her heel and hurried back to her car.

She was just easing off the handbrake when there came a rapping at the car window. With a sinking heart she saw it was Agatha. Reluctantly, Helen lowered the window.

'I really am so sorry,' said Agatha, who was not really sorry at all but was anxious to pick Helen's brains for more details about this bishop. 'I live down there in Lilac Lane. We can sit in the garden and have a chat. Say you forgive me.'

And poor Helen, who took her Christian duties seriously, felt she had to agree to a short visit.

* * *

Under the influence of a very strong gin and tonic combined with a comfortable chair in Agatha's garden, Helen began to relax.

Agatha talked about things that were going on in her village of Carsely and how it looked as if it was going to be a hot summer. She was just about to start asking questions about the bishop when Sir Charles Fraith strolled into the garden and sat down in a deck chair beside them.

'I thought I had asked you to return my keys,' said Agatha after she had made the introductions.

Charles gave a lazy smile. 'I saved you from leaving this nice garden to answer the door.'

'Where have you been?'

'Minding my own business, beloved. New reading, Agatha?' She had taken the parish magazine with her when she left the vicarage.

Agatha felt herself growing more and more irritated with Charles. She wanted the reality of this man who sometimes shared her bed to go away and let her nourish her new dream.

And yet there he sat at his ease, barbered and tailored to perfection. Agatha thought dismally that even when Charles was naked, he looked as if he was wearing a well-tailored skin.

'Mrs Toms gave it to me,' said Agatha. 'Helen here is hosting a party for the bishop.'

'To which I am sure I am invited,' said Charles, smiling at Helen.

'I will need to ask my husband,' said Helen, throwing a piteous look at Agatha.

'Really, Charles, you are pushy,' said Agatha. 'Helen and I were about to have a heart-to-heart before you butted in, so be a dear man and clear off.'

'No, no,' gasped Helen. 'Must go.' She was beginning to find Agatha rather terrifying. 'Bye.' And with that she fled.

'How did you get on?' was the first thing her husband demanded.

'She'll come,' said Helen. 'Oh, a friend of hers, Sir Charles Fraith, wanted an invitation but Agatha didn't want him there.'

Peregrine Toms was a snob and that title acted on him like magic. 'But he must come! I shall send him a card.'

'I could understand it,' Charles was saying, 'if you wanted to get your lustful hands under the purple, but you want to fall in lurv, Aggie. You always do and it always ends in misery.'

'At least I don't look at his bank balance. He's got an interesting face, that's all.'

Charles stifled a yawn. 'Now, why do I get a frisson of doom?'

Agatha studied the photograph of that face. What would it be like to be Mrs Bishop?

When she looked up from the magazine, she saw that Charles had fallen asleep.

What should she wear? Something classic. If the good weather held, maybe white chiffon. But one needed to be tall to wear floaty dresses and Agatha was only five feet five inches in her high heels. She went indoors and returned with a pile of fashion magazines and began to search through them.

Her mobile phone rang. Charles mumbled something but did not wake up. When Agatha answered it, she found an agitated Mrs Bloxby at the other end of the line.

'You really mustn't go to that party,' said Mrs Bloxby. 'I've found out something and I don't like it. Peter Salver-Hinkley was dating Jennifer Toynby, a local heiress. She disappeared a few years ago and hasn't been seen since. He was suspected of having had something to do with her disappearance but it never came to anything. But I think he might be dangerous. Leave him alone!'

'Oh, I think I should go,' said Agatha. 'I mean, I might do a bit of detecting and find out what happened to this Jennifer.'

'Please don't.'

'Look, you'll be there. You can stamp on my foot if you think I'm behaving badly. Bye.'

'But . . .'

Agatha hung up. A shadow fell across the magazine in front of her. She looked up at the sky. In the middle of the expanse of blue was one little round black cloud, blocking out the sun.

'And that do be a bad omen, lady,' said Charles suddenly in a stage gypsy voice.

Chapter Two

Agatha and her staff were so busy in the intervening weeks before the party that Agatha almost forgot about it. Sometimes the detective agency was quiet, but they had been suddenly swamped with demands to find lost animals and teenagers, proof for people wanting divorces and the inevitable find-the-shoplifter cases. She felt lucky to have such loyal and hardworking staff. There was young and beautiful Toni Gilmour, jester-faced Simon Black, ex-policeman Patrick Mulligan, gentle and elderly Phil Marshall, and secretary Mrs Freedman.

Helen had phoned once to say that Charles had not replied to his invitation, and that had reminded over-worked Agatha that she had not had time to buy a new outfit. But work had driven the adolescent dreams out of her head. It would be a boring sherry and nibbles affair.

She was not to know that the visit from a bishop to a forgotten place like Thirk Magna was the equivalent to

George Clooney volunteering to help at a sale of work. There seemed to be endless quarrelsome meetings about things like whether to hang out bunting.

Agatha Raisin would have been irritated to learn that two spinsters, the Dupin twins, nourished their own initial romantic dreams. They began to quarrel about the smallest things. Millicent accused the sexton of being vulgar because he wanted fairy lights at the entrance to the bell chamber, and he proved he could be really vulgar by telling her to stuff her bloody bells where the sun don't shine. Then Peregrine Toms caught a cold and the curate, Harry Mansfield, delivered the sermon the Sunday before the visit. His sermon was on love thy neighbour. He was a very good speaker and, by the time he had finished, hatchets were being mentally buried all over the village.

The church was built in the twelfth century. It was large for such a small village. But there had once been a castle, former home of Sir Randolph Quentin, the ruins of which could still be seen outside the village. The Quentin family had lost all their money in a series of crusades, and the church might have followed the castle into disuse had not the wealthy wool merchants of the Cotswolds given generously to its upkeep and improvement.

Perhaps Julian Brody alone was not moved to charity by the sermon. He was worried about Helen. She had a purple bruise on one cheek and Julian suspected her nasty husband had put it there. He slipped out of the church before the service was over and made his way to the vicarage next door. He knew the door wasn't locked during the day and so he walked in boldly and followed the sound of a television set. Peregrine was in his study watching the racing from Cheltenham, a whisky in one hand and a cigar in the other. Julian took out his phone and, before Peregrine became aware he was in the room, snapped a photograph. Startled by the flash, Peregrine swivelled his head and yelled, 'What do you think you are doing?'

'If you strike your wife again,' said Julian, 'I shall post up this photograph all over the village and put it on Twitter.'

'I'm a sick man,' wailed Peregrine.

'You are indeed. Get yourself a good psychiatrist, you horrible creature.'

After Julian had left, Peregrine thought hard. Helen must get that photo for him. Next time he struck her, he'd make sure the marks didn't show.

Said the bishop to the dean, Donald Whitby, 'Why on earth did I say I would go to – what's the name of the place?'

'Thirk Magna,' said the dean. 'And you have got to go. There's a bit about your visit in the local paper. Besides, you told me you wanted to meet that detective.'

'Changed my mind. She's probably as hard as nails.'

Julian was sharing a candlelit dinner with Helen Toms at a new French restaurant in Mircester. It had been

Helen's invitation, and his preliminary elation was dampened by the thought that her horrible husband had probably given her orders to steal his camera and erase that photograph.

He chatted amiably about this and that until the end of the meal when he leaned across the table and took her hand in his. 'Don't go home tonight,' he said.

Her face turned pale but she said in a little voice, 'All right.'

'No, the bastard is not having that photograph, but if you go home and tell him that, he will beat you up. My aunt, Maggie, lives near here in Mircester and she will put you up for the night. I bought you some stuff from Marks to change into. Peregrine can't do anything until the bishop's gone and then I will be there to see he doesn't.'

She gently drew her hand away. 'I cannot love you, Julian. I wish I could.'

'You might come to. But stay with my aunt. Peregrine will think you are seducing me. I will give you the photo after I print off several copies. He will be so delighted he will behave well.'

Banks of leaves and flowers were between the tables and so neither Helen nor Julian saw the Dupin twins pay their bill and hurry out.

'It is our duty to tell the dear vicar,' said Millicent. 'When you went to the lavatory, I could distinctly hear her agreeing to spend the night with him and then that Edith Piaf music started up again. But I heard that bit.'

'I think you should leave it until tomorrow,' said Mavis.

'No. Tonight. He will be worried when she doesn't

come home and may even call the police. As leaders of this community, it is our duty.'

'Well, do it yourself,' said Mavis.

But Helen had decided not to stay with Julian's aunt. So, all Millicent got for her interference was a bruise on her cheek to match Helen's as the infuriated vicar punched her hard. 'I shall report you to the police,' shouted Millicent. 'You have struck a Dupin!'

Detective Sergeant Bill Wong, accompanied by a new detective, Larry Jensen, was just passing the front desk in Mircester police station when they heard Mavis and her sister putting in a complaint about the vicar of Thirk Magna. 'How he could behave so badly when the dear bishop is due to visit?' shouted Mavis. 'He laid hands on a Dupin!'

To Bill's surprise, Larry said to the desk sergeant, 'I'll take this.'

Bill said good night and went off to meet his fiancée, Detective Constable Alice Peterson, who was waiting for him in the pub. Bill was half-Chinese and half-British, which gave him an attractive look, but he was unaware of it and he considered Larry to be much too handsome to be around Alice. He hoped Larry would forget the invitation to join them for a drink, but only five minutes after Bill had joined Alice, Larry walked into the pub.

Larry had thick, fair hair and very blue eyes. His features were regular and he was lightly tanned having just got back from a Spanish holiday.

'That sounded like a domestic,' said Bill. 'Not like you to get involved.'

'Tell you about it sometime,' said Larry.

Agatha had again forgotten about the bishop's visit and let out a squawk of alarm when Mrs Bloxby, the vicar's wife, turned up on her doorstep, prepared to accompany her to Thirk Magna.

'I haven't anything to wear,' fretted Agatha.

'Nonsense. You've loads of clothes.'

'But the weather's perfect. I'd always imagined myself wearing something chiffon and floaty and a big straw hat.'

'It is a small event,' said the vicar's wife. 'The bishop will stay about half an hour. What about that pale green silk trouser suit you bought recently?'

'If I can find it.'

'In your wardrobe?'

'I can't remember taking it out of its bag,' wailed Agatha. 'I hope I didn't put it in the rubbish.'

By dint of not telling Agatha that she had called to collect her an hour early, expecting the usual dithering, Mrs Bloxby was able to get her to Thirk Magna just as the bishop's car was arriving.

The bells were sending cascades of sound over the village. *Pom, pom, pom, pom, POM!* Agatha could feel the ground beneath her feet reverberating to the sound. The bishop's chauffeur jumped out and opened the door of the limousine. The Right Reverend Peter

Salver-Hinkley emerged, dressed in a long purple cassock. He was hatless and a little breeze ruffled his glossy black curls. From the other side of the limo came the dean Donald Whitby, a thickset man in a white robe and highly decorated stole.

'Mrs Raisin! Your mouth is hanging open!' shouted Mrs Bloxby, unfortunately as the sounds of the last *pom* died away.

The Dupin twins were racing down from the bell tower. Millicent stuck out her foot and tripped Mavis up. Mavis writhed on the ground, screaming with rage. Agatha moved forward to welcome the bishop but the vicar, Peregrine Toms, got there first. He held out his hand but Millicent ducked under it and cried, 'Welcome! Welcome! I am Millicent Dupin.'

The bishop was tall. He smiled across at Agatha and said, 'And who is this lady?'

'Place is full of rubberneckers,' said Peregrine. 'Come up to the vicarage. I am sure you could do with a drink.'

'Is that Alf Bloxby?' said Peter, ignoring him. 'Who is this lady, Alf?'

'That is Agatha Raisin from our village. Oh, meet my wife.'

'You must come to dinner and bring the famous detective with you. I have heard of you, Mrs Raisin.'

'Agatha, please.'

Agatha Raisin felt like a love-struck teenager. 'Let's find a drink,' said the bishop, tucking her arm in his and walking up the short drive to the vicarage, deaf to a loud wail of 'Trollop!' from Millicent.

Oh, dear, thought Mrs Bloxby. Mrs Raisin is about to plunge into another obsession. Where is Sir Charles? He might tease her out of it.

It is doubtful if so many women had ever hated Agatha Raisin so much all at once, and Agatha was human enough to relish their jealousy. But was this gorgeous bishop gay? He appeared to have a lithe, muscular figure under that cassock. Agatha became aware that the dean, Donald Whitby, was trying to get his attention by clutching at Peter's sleeve.

'What is it?' demanded Peter, coming to such an abrupt stop that Agatha teetered on her very high heels.

'The Dupin sisters are the queens of this hamlet,' hissed Donald, 'and you pretty much nearly cut them dead. One of them has begun to cry.'

'Sorry, Agatha,' said the bishop, smiling down at her. 'Mustn't let you lure me away. We'll talk later.'

Agatha watched him approach the twins. Mavis was the one who had burst into tears. Peter handed her his handkerchief and she clutched it to her bosom.

'Had they met him before?' asked Agatha.

'Not as far as I know. It is like an Elvis Presley fan suddenly meeting him face-to-face for the first time.'

'Need to die to do that. Oh, look who's here.'

Charles came strolling up. 'I've never seen so many besotted women, including you, Aggie. What's the big attraction?'

'He is sexy,' said Agatha.

'I think he's dangerous. Looked up that old case, Jennifer Toynby. She was a rich heiress. Disappeared from a party at the bishop's palace one evening. Never seen again.'

'Was the bishop suspected of anything?'

'No. People said it was thought he was going to marry her. There was even a rumour going around that they had got as far as the lawyer's, hers that is, to discuss marriage settlements. Maybe he felt huffed, feeling the glory of his purple position in the church was above sordid money. Maybe . . . oh, here he comes with two women who have just stepped out of a medieval fresco scuttling after him.'

Agatha suddenly felt sorry for the Dupin twins. They had obviously bought new outfits which surely matched everything else they still had in their wardrobes. Mircester boasted a couple of 'lady' shops, mostly featuring two-piece outfits in drab colours. Despite the heat of the early evening, Millicent was wearing a wool cardigan over a silk blouse and she had a wool skirt to match, all in a sort of sludge colour. Mavis was bolder in an ankle-length, deep purple dress, but it was cut too low, exposing a flat, freckled bosom.

Agatha quickly caught Charles by the arm as he was trying to escape and deftly introduced him to the Dupin twins. The magic sound of a title stopped both in their tracks as the sisters began to vie for Charles's attention.

'Every time I try to get a moment with you,' complained the bishop, 'someone always interrupts. Oh, what is it, Peregrine?'

'Perhaps you would like something stronger than champagne?'

'This is like the Mad Hatter's tea party. I am not drinking champagne, I am not drinking anything. Be a dear chap and fetch me a whisky – and you, Mrs Raisin?'

'Agatha, please. Gin and tonic.'

Peregrine stalked off and could soon be heard yelling for his wife.

'Is there a lot of that in the church?' asked Agatha.

'What? Alcohol?'

'No. Wife beating. The vicar there beats his wife. Will you have a word with him?'

'He will simply deny it and beat her harder. *She* has to do something about it. Dear Agatha. I love your outfit. You look as cool as a green salad. Have dinner with me tomorrow?'

'That, may I remind you, will be Sunday.'

'Evening's free. The dean will handle anything. Eight o'clock? Give me your card and I'll pick you up.'

'All right,' said Agatha noticing the twins bearing down on them. 'If you do one thing for me. Be nice to the Dupin twins.'

The bishop's obvious admiration of her had given the not usually kind or charitable Agatha a desire to spread happiness.

To her relief, he smiled and nodded and gave his full attention to the twins. Charles drew Agatha away. 'You are missing all the gorgeous eats in the drawing room. Some French chef conjured them up.'

'Lead the way,' said Agatha. 'Tell me about marriage settlements.'

'Oh, come on! You, a bishop's wife?'

'Not me. He was romancing some heiress who disappeared and was never found. I'm interested.'

'Don't be, unless someone is paying you.'

'Well, it would make a change from the usual dull routine.' Agatha stood still suddenly at the door to the vicarage. 'Something's wrong here,' she whispered.

'Instead of standing there feeling all intuitive, why don't you go in?'

The French windows to the drawing room had been left open wide to allow guests easy access that way. Two waitresses were circling guests with plates of canapés and glasses of champagne.

Agatha quickly located the source of her unease. In a far corner stood a handsome man snarling something in a low voice at the vicar. Beside them stood Helen Toms. She looked on the verge of tears. Agatha sailed forward. 'Helen!' she cried. 'Just the lady I want to see.'

She put a firm clasp on Helen's arm and drew her away. Agatha escorted Helen out to the lawn and said, 'What's going on? You're white and miserable! Who's the handsome fellow?'

'Julian Brody.'

'Aha! The one who got his friend to cater, otherwise you would have had to do it?'

'Yes,' mumbled Helen.

She was wearing a light chiffon stole. A sudden gust of wind blew it half off her shoulders, exposing black bruises on both her upper arms, as if she had been forcefully held down . . . ?

Agatha could feel fury mounting inside her. 'Hey, bishop?' she called.

Peter came hurrying up with the twins scrambling after him. 'Would you give your blessing to a man who rapes his wife?' demanded Agatha.

'Of course not. I'd report him to the police.'

'But what if the wife was too intimidated to back up any charge?'

'What would you do, Agatha? Do tell us,' said the bishop, suddenly not wanting to be drawn into some vicar's domestic mess.

'I'd kill him,' said Agatha. 'Someone ought to kill Peregrine Toms.'

There was a startled silence.

'Our vicar is all that is good and kind,' said Mavis.

'And I'd bash the head in of anyone supporting him,' said Agatha, enjoying the freedom of being rude, bad and horrible to know. She had already drunk two very large gin and tonics on an empty stomach. The effects now seemed to be evaporating fast and she noticed the lurking distaste in the bishop's eyes, the whiteness of Helen's face, and wondered if she had temporarily run mad. But Peregrine had to be stopped.

She was all too soon to regret her championship of Helen who mumbled that now Agatha had just made everything worse. The bishop with a small Dupin twin on either side of him, like two tugs towing a purple liner into harbour, smiled at Agatha and said, 'I am so sorry. I have another engagement this Sunday that I quite forgot about. I will phone you next time I am free.' He strode off.

'Now look what you've done!' said Agatha to Helen.

Helen burst into tears. 'Why is it always my fault?' she shouted. 'To hell with you, you interfering bag!'

'Let's go,' said Charles. 'You were pretty awful, Aggie, but I have to admit this lot are worse than you any day. Your bishop has feet of clay. Rattle, rattle, rattle. He's probably gay anyway and beats up his dean.'

'Only on Sundays,' said an amused voice behind him. Charles swung round and found himself facing the dean. 'Are you going to punish the vicar, Sir Charles?'

'Going to castrate him,' said Charles. 'Let's go, Aggie.'

'Don't call me Aggie!'

The bishop narrowed his eyes as he watched them leave. Agatha, he noticed, had very long legs and a high bottom. Maybe he'd reissue that invitation. The whole thing was a bore. He decided to leave.

'I don't want you to go near the Tomses again,' said Charles, sprawling on the sofa in Agatha's cottage. 'Helen Toms is the sort of woman who creates murderers. I mean, that lawyer is obviously besotted with her.'

'No one is besotted with me,' said Agatha. 'You heard the bishop cancelling our date.'

Agatha's phone rang. 'I'll get it,' said Charles. 'Who are you not at home to?'

'Everyone.'

Wondering, not for the first time, why Agatha had had

the phone installed in her hallway with extensions in the kitchen and in her bedroom but nothing in the sitting room, Charles answered the shrill ringing.

'May I speak to Mrs Raisin?'

'I am afraid she is out this evening.'

'This is Peter Salver-Hinkley. To whom am I speaking?'

'Her fiancé, Charles Fraith.'

'Ah, yes. We met. Tell her I am free on Sunday after all and I will collect her at eight o'clock.'

'I won't tell her. Good evening.'

Agatha looked up as Charles entered the sitting room. 'Who was it?'

'Double-glazing salesman,' said Charles.

But Charles in his lazy way forgot all about his lies so it was a startled Agatha who opened the door on Sunday evening to find the bishop on the doorstep.

'Dinner?' said Peter. 'Didn't your fiancé tell you?'

'I haven't got a fiancé.'

'Charles Fraith?'

'Definitely not.'

'Right. Let's go.'

'I'm not suitably dressed,' said Agatha, who was wearing an old housedress.

The bishop grinned. 'Then slip on something tight and let's go.'

Agatha appeared back downstairs in record time in a fuchsia chiffon blouse with a high frill at the neck and a pair of black velvet trousers. She had not worn the blouse before but felt it was the right combination of flattering colour and yet rather prim lines.

She thought she noticed a startled gleam of lechery in Peter's eyes but decided it must be a trick of the light. 'There's a new restaurant in Mircester,' said Peter. 'Greek. Supposed to be pretty good.'

'I hope the food is hot enough. I was in Greece last year and everything served seemed to be tepid.'

'Ah, you innocents abroad,' mocked Peter. 'Always stick with the other tourists.'

'Don't patronise me,' said Agatha sharply.

Shouldn't have asked her out, thought Peter. Hard as marble. Oh, well. Quick bite to eat. Call my chauffeur to take her home and get rid of her quick.

The restaurant had a car park at the back. He helped Agatha out of the car. Greek music was blaring from loudspeakers. A young man dressed as an Evzone, a Greek ceremonial guard, was marching up and down clutching a toy rifle.

'They always look as if they are wearing white tutus and about to dance *Swan Lake*. Very touristy-looking place,' added Agatha maliciously.

But Peter had decided that Agatha was definitely a waste of space and just wanted the evening to end quickly. 'Oh, but they do say the food is good.'

When they walked into the restaurant, they were seated at a table opposite a large mirror. Because the evening was warm, she had not bothered to wear a jacket or coat and noticed for the first time that her new blouse was transparent, showing her frilly black brassiere underneath. She turned almost the same colour as her blouse and hissed, 'Lend me your jacket.'

'Why?' he demanded, deliberately obtuse.

'There's an underslip that goes with this damned blouse and I forgot to put it on.'

'Oh, very well.' He took off his white linen jacket and passed it over to her. 'I will order for us.'

Agatha wanted to say sharply that she preferred to choose what she would eat herself but she was still too embarrassed about her see-through blouse to protest. They started with dolmades, followed by moussaka, both dishes being tepid. He ordered a carafe of retsina, a wine that tasted to Agatha like paint stripper. Agatha asked for some ordinary red wine instead.

'Any interesting cases at the moment?' he asked.

His beautiful face was a study in anticipated boredom and Agatha found herself saying, 'Funnily enough, it's not one of my cases. It's about that disappearing heiress, Jennifer Toynby.'

'What on earth has that got to do with you?'

'It is such a *glamorous* mystery,' said Agatha. 'I mean, a bishop, an heiress, and all that. Rumour has it you were going to be married.'

'Rubbish. She contributed a good bit to the church and my dean persuaded me to squire her about a bit. She had a boyfriend, Lawrence Crowther, a great hulking bull of a farmer. Now, they were about to get engaged just before she disappeared. Excuse me.'

He took out his phone and walked a little way away

32

from the table, raising his voice to try to be heard above the loudspeakers now belting out 'Zorba the Greek'.

The waiter politely turned down the volume just as the bishop was saying, 'Yes, John, I want you to bring the limo round and take my guest back to Carsely.' He dropped his voice, but Agatha heard him say urgently, 'Bored out of my skull, dear boy. Oh, you are just around the corner? Good, that's great.'

Now, Agatha Raisin had been insulted by experts, but never before had anyone said they found her boring. Although middle-aged, she felt suddenly young and insecure. Agatha had always rated her looks as low, and it did not dawn on her that her questions were annoying him.

'We were talking about the missing heiress,' said Agatha when he had sat down again.

'You were. I wasn't. Oh, here is my driver with the car. I must beg you to leave me with the bill and then I have to rush home to deal with an urgent matter.'

It was only when Agatha was finally dropped outside his cottage that she realised she was still wearing his jacket.

She was somehow grateful to Charles. Had she anticipated the invitation, she would have begun to weave rosy fantasies. As it was, she could face up to the fact that he was an arrogant man with a beautiful face, but eminently forgettable.

Chapter Three

Occasionally, in the weeks that followed, Agatha thought briefly about the bishop. Charles wanted to know about her date, but Agatha only said that her question about a missing heiress had seemed to rattle him. There was a lot of work still pouring into the agency and so her mind was soon taken up with other things, one of those being the return to Carsely of her ex-husband, James Lacey. He was a travel writer and often absent. He lived next door to her and called on her two days after he got back.

Agatha was always taken aback at how handsome he was when she had not seen him for some time. He was tall with thick black hair going grey at the sides, and with bright blue eyes in a tanned face. Agatha as usual reminded herself that the label chauvinist pig applied to James.

'Have you eaten yet?' he asked.

'Haven't had a chance,' said Agatha. 'Just got home.'

'I've got a free voucher to a Greek restaurant in Mircester,' said James. 'Like to try it? Dinner for two.'

'Been there,' said Agatha. 'Cold food and sour wine.'

'It says it's under "new management".'

'Oh, well, I was about to defrost a hamburger. You're on.' Agatha was just getting into James's car when Charles came hurrying up.

'Where are you off to?'

'Greek restaurant,' said James.

'Can I come too?' asked Charles. 'Nobody loves me.'

'I can understand why,' mocked James, 'if you keep trying to push your way into other people's dates. Oh, hop in.'

The first person Agatha noticed on entering the restaurant was the bishop, who was treating the two Dupin sisters to dinner. Why? Money, thought Agatha. 'Charles,' she said aloud, 'we all know you chase women who've got money.'

'Keep your voice down, you horrible thing,' hissed Charles.

'What prompted that?' asked James curiously.

'Over there is the Bishop of Mircester,' said Charles.

'You mean the Greek god and two frumps?'

'Cruel, but yes.'

'Why would an unmarried bishop take out two ladies like that for dinner?' asked Agatha.

'I neither know nor care,' said James. 'Order some food, Agatha.'

* * *

'Oh, there's that hard-faced detective creature,' said Mavis Dupin.

Peter Salver-Hinkley looked across the restaurant. Agatha Raisin seemed to be keeping two men entertained. He recognised Charles from the village party. Who was the other man?

As if in answer to his thoughts, Mavis said, 'The handsome one is her ex-husband, James Lacey.'

'Wasn't there some scandal about their marriage?'

'Oh, yes,' said Mavis eagerly. 'The first time they tried to get married, Agatha's husband turned up. She had forgotten to tell everyone she was still married. Then he was murdered.'

'Of course,' said the bishop. 'It was all over the newspapers. But they got married anyway and then split up. She is attractive.'

'Oh, go along with you.' Mavis gave him what was meant to be a playful punch on the arm but it nearly knocked him out of his chair. 'She's got such small eyes, hasn't she, Millicent?'

'I've got a teddy bear with eyes like that,' said Millicent.

The Raisin woman's got a whole cupboard full of skeletons, thought the bishop. I shouldn't have been in such a hurry to brush her off.

Charles said, 'I don't like the look of this place. There's a good Italian place round the corner. Let's go there.'

'Oh, all right,' said Agatha.

'Wait a minute,' said James crossly. 'I wanted Greek food and I still want it.'

36

'I've eaten here before,' said Agatha. 'You've heard of chicken in a basket? Well this is yuk in a bucket.'

'I am surprised you want to leave, considering the fact that the Greek god over there seems fascinated by you.'

Agatha followed his gaze. Peter smiled and nodded. Agatha gave a chilly little nod back.

'So, who is he?' asked James.

'He was nearly Agatha's latest squeeze,' said Charles. 'He took her out for dinner to this very restaurant but our Aggie starts to nose into his guilty past and so he freezes her out.'

'Not surprised,' said James. 'Why did he ask you in the first place? What? Did I say something wrong?'

'Oh, no,' said Charles. 'Clumsy as an ox as usual. Our Aggie fascinates fellows. They drop at her feet. See what I mean? The bish is heading this way.'

'Good evening, Agatha,' said Peter. 'You still have my jacket.'

'I kept meaning to send it to you,' said Agatha. 'Oh, you don't know James. James, Peter Salver-Hinkley, Bishop of Mircester. Peter, James Lacey.'

'You are that famous travel writer,' said Peter. He pulled out a chair and sat down.

'Are yiz ready tae order?' demanded a hairy, thickset waiter.

'And I thought it was Edinburgh that used to be called the Athens of the North and not Glasgow,' said Charles.

'Here, mac! You takin' the piss?'

'No, he's just being silly,' said James quickly. 'Do

excuse us, Peter, but I am really hungry and your ladies are waiting for you. Agatha, what would you like?'

'I won't have a starter,' said Agatha. 'They've actually got fish and chips. Oh, and anything but retsina.'

'I'll have the same,' said Charles.

James shrugged and said he would settle for one dish as well but ordered moussaka.

To James's dismay, the Dupin sisters came over and pulled up chairs at his table, squeezing in on either side of the bishop.

'Isn't this cozy,' said Charles, his eyes alight with mischief.

'Dear ladies,' said Peter, 'I was just about to rejoin you.'

Sharp and bony Dupin knees pressed in on either side of his legs. He scowled. The only reason he had asked them out was because they had hinted they would give money to the abbey. He stood up abruptly. 'I've just remembered. I am expecting an important phone call. Do forgive me.' And with that, he fled from the restaurant.

'Well, really!' exclaimed Millicent. 'You must have said something rude, Mrs Raisin. We heard you are famous for your rudeness.'

'Nothing I have ever said could begin to compete with you two witches. So, bugger off,' said Agatha gleefully.

As the outraged sisters fled to their table, James said, 'That was unwarranted, Agatha.'

'Oh, come on, James,' said Charles. 'They were flashing warrant cards.'

'But Agatha always attracts men,' said James, 'and those two haven't a hope in hell. You should be more charitable, Agatha.'

Charles saw Agatha smiling fondly at James because of his remark and suddenly felt bad-tempered. 'What the hell is this?' he demanded as the waiter put a slate with a greasy pile of fish and chips in front of him. 'Why the slate? Am I supposed to write a comment on this heap of grease?'

'Lissen here, mac,' growled the waiter. 'I dinnae cook the stuff. So, eat it or shut up.'

'Mine is the same,' said Agatha. 'Take it away and give it to your twenty-five children.'

The waiter stared at her. James clenched his fists. Then the incredible happened. The waiter began to laugh. He said when he had finished laughing, 'You're no' frae Glesca, are ye, hen?'

'No, and they wouldn't dare serve muck like this.'

The waiter placed a chair next to Agatha and sat down. He poured himself a glass of wine and said, 'On the hoose.'

Charles opened his mouth to protest but Agatha kicked him under the table. With one of her odd flashes of intuition, she said to the waiter, 'You know who I am and you've got something to tell me about our bishop.'

Agatha translated the waiter's tale in her head into standard English. What it amounted to was that the bishop had brought the now missing heiress, Jennifer Toynby, to the restaurant. The waiter had heard them arguing; he was not serving their table that evening but he said dramatically that when she had gone to the toilet, the bishop had looked after her with murder in his eyes.

'Why does he bring people here?' asked Agatha.

'He has shares in this place, see?' said the waiter. 'Here comes the boss.'

The boss was as low-browed and tattooed as the waiter. He gave a curt nod. Their waiter said, 'He says if yiz goes tae the Napoli in the square, it's on the hoose.'

Agatha slipped the waiter a hefty tip as she wanted to interrogate him further when she was on her own.

James wanted to go home but Charles pointed out that the Napoli had a good reputation and a free meal was a free meal. What Charles had not explained was that the Napoli was mostly a takeaway pizza parlour with only two tables in a corner.

The menu showed a list of pizzas, spaghetti bolognaise and lasagne. There was no drinks licence. 'No wonder it's a free meal,' grumbled James.

'What puzzles me,' said Agatha, 'is why our bishop should involve his business affair with a Greek restaurant.'

'Probably launders money,' said Charles. 'His adopted family are rich, made their money in steel in the days when steel was worth something, and I doubt if he has any morals at all.'

'So why go into the church?'

'Power. Besides, he gets to dress up. Nice robes.'

James said, 'It seems as if you are supposed to go up to the counter and order what you want. Let's scrub it.'

40

'I never scrub a free meal,' said Charles. 'Come on. Orders, please.'

'Tell you what,' said James. 'I brought some nice wine back from Italy. Let's take the meal to my place.'

After they had finished eating and James was clearing away the dishes, Charles said, 'Stop dreaming about exposing the bish as a murderer, Aggie.'

'Don't call me Aggie. Why not?'

'You are not being paid to investigate.'

'Humour me. Tell me about the missing heiress. You are bound to have known her, in your heiress hunting.'

'Tall girl. Big nose, small mouth, big hands and feet, dyed blonde hair but oh, that laugh. Enough to make any man want to strangle her. She actually laughed – haw, haw, haw – so loud she could have been heard all over Mircester. I'm not joking. The wedding was all set when she suddenly disappeared. Distraught parents. Peter on television looking noble, offering a fifty-thousand-pound award.'

'Now, that's interesting,' said Agatha, her bearlike eyes gleaming.

'What is?' asked James, carrying in a tray of coffee.

'The fact that Peter should offer a large award for information leading to the finding of his fiancée,' said Agatha. 'I think he's mean so I reckon he knew damn well she wasn't going to be found.'

'She wasn't his fiancée. In fact, she was expected to marry some farming chap,' said James.

41

'I'd forgotten that,' said Agatha. 'Name was Lawrence something or other.'

'I'm bored,' said Charles. 'What about bed, Agatha?'

'Just as long as it isn't mine,' snapped Agatha.

'Forget the whole thing,' said James. 'No one is paying you to investigate.'

'You're right,' said Agatha. 'Our bishop is a waste of space.'

But she did not know then that one insult would change her mind.

A busy volume of work in the following weeks kept the bishop from her thoughts. One sunny Saturday morning, Mrs Bloxby called on Agatha.

'I am worried about the Dupin sisters,' said the vicar's wife. 'Peter Salver-Hinkley is making trouble there. If you are free, we could visit Helen Toms and find out more.'

'What sort of trouble?'

'I think he is getting money from them. They are supposed to be very rich. But I think they get money from a trust fund and what was generous when they were younger won't go very far now.'

'What could I do?' asked Agatha.

'You could warn them.'

'I don't carry any weight.'

'Oh, do help.'

* * *

Helen Toms greeted them with a sunny smile. She said the vicar was resting and suggested they have tea in the garden. She exuded an air of triumph, thought Agatha. Funny atmosphere.

'I'll go to the toilet first,' said Agatha.

'Me, too,' said Mrs Bloxby, feeling she needed Agatha's support when finally asking Helen for *her* support in confronting the Dupins.

'Help!' came a faint cry from behind a door on Agatha's left. She tried to open the door, but it was locked.

Mrs Bloxby pointed to a large key lying on a small table outside the door. Agatha inserted the key in the lock and opened the door. Peregrine Toms, the vicar, was bound to a chair in front of a desk. There was caked blood from a wound on the back of his head.

Agatha reached for her phone. 'No!' he cried. 'The shame of it.'

Ignoring him, Agatha asked for police and ambulance services. 'Did your wife do this?' she asked.

'It was Mavis Dupin. She crept up and hit me,' he said. 'I will never live this down. Why did you call the police, you interfering old bag?'

Agatha was just about to untie his bindings but now she withdrew her hands and said, 'Better the police see you as you are.'

'Interfering cow. I'll get you for this.'

Agatha slowly turned round. She could swear the temperature in the room had suddenly dropped. Mavis Dupin was standing in the doorway.

'I've called the police and ambulance,' said Agatha. 'You've got some explaining to do.'

'We were playing a game,' wailed Mavis. 'It's called Bondage. Isn't that right, vicar?'

'How do you explain that nasty wound on his head?'

'It was an accident,' said Peregrine. 'I fell and bumped my head on the desk.'

'Now then. What's all this?'

Policeman Larry Jensen stood in the doorway. 'I see the reverend is tied up with a bash on his head. Who did this?'

The vicar and Mavis stated a chorus of it being just a game and that Agatha had insisted on dramatizing the situation.

Mrs Bloxby's cool voice sounded. 'When Mrs Raisin and I entered the vicarage, we heard a cry for help coming from this room. The door was locked. We unlocked it with a key I found on the table outside. We found the vicar in this state.'

'I am a Dupin,' said Mavis, throwing her head so far back that all could see up the famous Dupin nose. 'I never lie. Peregrine and I were playing a game called Bondage. It is perfectly respectable and is played at parties at the bishop's palace.'

Larry's eyes gleamed. He earned extra money by leaking stories to the press. This one could be gold. He saw the shrewd assessing look in Agatha's eyes and said hurriedly, 'As this is a police investigation, Mrs Raisin, wait outside and take your friend with you.'

'You will need our statements,' said Agatha.

'Yes, yes. Later.'

But Larry was foiled by the arrival of the paramedics. And suddenly the room was full of people: Helen bending over her husband; Bishop Peter Salver-Hinkley talking intensely to Mavis and Millicent Dupin and the rest of the bell ringers.

Agatha and Mrs Bloxby had retreated to the front lawn where they were joined by the lawyer, Julian Brody. 'Did you encourage Mavis to bash the vicar?' demanded Agatha.

Julian sighed. He looked down the sunny lawn and over to the green wold dotted with sheep that lay on the other side. 'No, I did not,' he said finally. 'The bishop moves amongst us like a fallen angel. I think he put the Dupin sisters up to this.'

'Helen seemed to be enjoying herself,' said Agatha.

'Nonsense!' he said firmly. And then that sigh came again. 'I keep my hand in by doing a bit of conveyancing,' said Julian. 'I inherited quite a lot of money from an uncle and left London. The Cotswold dream. Then along comes our bishop and the show is over and I am left on the stage in the middle of the badly painted scenery with a load of stock characters. Evil bishop, beaten wife turning into a bitchy doormat, spinster twins and bells, bells, bells. And the rest of the bell ringers are types that can be found in London.'

'Geography is no escape,' said Mrs Bloxby. 'You are like someone who goes on a beach holiday to Thailand

and thinks if only life could be like this all year round. Inherits money, goes off with family, then one month in, teenager's on drugs and wife's off with a local and then he gets a tropical disease. Misery can happen anywhere, Mr Brody.'

Julian gave a reluctant laugh. 'What a Pickwickian summary of disaster. Here's the ambulance. My cottage is just next door. Let's go there. Gin, I think. It's a gin day.'

Agatha beamed, noticing for the first time how good-looking he was with his curly black hair and tanned face. And if you went out with him, came a nasty little thought, wouldn't Charles just hate it.

Mrs Bloxby was glad they were going to Julian's house. She shrewdly guessed that he was not the type to raise a new obsession in Agatha's breast.

They sat in Julian's garden, slumped lazily in deck chairs. Great fleecy clouds sailed overhead. 'There you are, Mrs Bloxby,' said Julian, pointing to the clouds. 'That's what happens to sheep when they die.'

No reply, for Mrs Bloxby had fallen asleep.

'I'm interested in what's been going on here,' said Agatha, keeping her voice low so as not to wake her friend.

'We were going on as usual,' said Julian, his voice sounding weary. 'Cling, clang, clong go the bells. We occasionally squabble, I chase Helen, and Gloria chases me. I felt I had freed my princess. I took a photo of the vicar drinking and smoking at his desk when he said he was ill, and threatened to put it on the notice board at the church if he hit his wife again. I think he made sure next time he didn't mark her and she refused to tell me anything and along came the bish. I'm guessing but I think he got Helen to tell the truth. Then he wound up the Dupins to play bondage games. He may even have suggested that a good beating might even the score. He was seen walking and talking with Helen and she began to look radiant.'

'Of course she did,' said Agatha. 'These weak women are nothing if not manipulative.'

'Has anyone ever told you how horrible you are?' asked Julian.

'Often. May I have another G and T? Don't look so mutinous. I'll tell you how we'll get the bishop away from Helen.'

'I will keep you to that. One G and T coming up. Ice? There you are. Now, how do we do it?'

'That heiress who disappeared. Wouldn't you just like to find out that it was our bishop who got rid of her?'

'Of course. But how? I am sure the police tried.'

'But not hard enough. As no one is paying me to find out, you will need to lie and hint at a mysterious donor of massive funds to find out what happened to the girl.'

'Dammit, I will pay you.'

'Thank you. Call at my office on Monday morning

and sign the contracts, and we will discuss time and payment then.'

Agatha woke Mrs Bloxby and suggested they leave. Julian waved them good-bye and then frowned as he saw a group of bell ringers bearing down on him. In the lead came the sexton and the butcher followed by the schoolteacher and the divorcée, Gloria.

'You've got to help us to stop that damned bishop from coming here,' said the sexton, Harry Bury. 'T'ain't fair the way he messes things up. The Dupin girls are all in a flutter. He keeps visiting them and so they miss rehearsals whilst they twitter about.' He raised his voice in shrill mockery, '"Oh, do have some of our seedcake, bishop." I'd take their seedcake and shove it up their arses.'

'No room for it, ducks,' said Gloria. 'Our dear bishop is already up there and taken up all the space.'

Agatha turned around at the bottom of the garden. A breeze had sprung up and cloud shadows chased across the lawn and across the angry faces surrounding Julian. And there was Peter, in the vicarage garden next door, well aware of all the jealousy and fuss. Suddenly aware of a premonition of some sort of danger, Agatha began to wish she had never agreed to take on the case for Julian. She heard footsteps behind her and swung around. Charles came hurrying up. 'Leaving?' he asked.

'I'll just have a word with Peter,' said Agatha, and Mrs Bloxby supressed a groan. But to Agatha's annoyance, Charles showed no sign of either following her or of being jealous. The bishop saw her coming, detached himself from the eager Dupins, and approached her, the sun shining on the purple silk of his tunic.

'I really do owe you a decent meal,' he said. 'You must have been wondering about my dreadful taste in restaurants. Actually, I've got money invested in that wretched place. But it'll pay if I ever get a decent manager. Now, what about dinner at Harry's?'

Harry's was a very good restaurant, specialising in steaks.

'All right,' said Agatha. 'When?'

'Well, what about tonight?'

'Peter!' came a wail from behind them. 'You are coming to us for dinner tonight!'

He turned the blast of his charm on the twins whose brogues had made no sound on the grass as they had sidled up to hear what he was talking about. 'My poor old brain. How can you forgive me? Agatha. I will phone you.'

'Do that,' said Agatha grumpily, because she saw that Gloria, the bell-ringing divorcée, had joined Charles and was hanging onto his arm. 'Coming, Charles?' she said, and then walked off with Mrs Bloxby, fully expecting him to follow. But when she reached her car and turned around, he had strolled off in the other direction with Gloria and not once did he look back.

* * *

49

After Agatha had dropped her friend off at the vicarage, she drove home slowly. She was hungry, but, somehow, she had put about an inch on her waistline. 'And how did that happen?' she asked aloud as she got out of her car. To her surprise, Detective Sergeant Bill Wong and Detective Constable Alice Peterson were waiting for her.

'What's up?' asked Agatha. 'Is Charles all right?' So she is keen on Charles, thought Bill. When the police call, the first person feared for is the dearest.

'Shall we go inside?' said Bill aloud.

'Go through to the garden. You know the way. I've got fresh lemonade. Like some?'

'Maybe later. Homemade lemonade! You're becoming a true villager.'

It could be argued that, in a way, Agatha was becoming more like a village lady, having bought a pint of the lemonade in the village shop that morning along with several other villagers who were no doubt also claiming it as their own. Lying somehow increased with the good weather, as if lies, like flowers, had been dormant all winter.

Agatha felt relaxed, if curious. She had just dropped off Mrs Bloxby, it wasn't Charles, so . . .

'James!' she exclaimed. 'Never tell me something has happened to James.'

'Stop running through the names of the few people you actually care about,' said Bill. 'Do you remember being on the scene when the vicar, Peregrine Toms, was found with his head bashed?'

'Yes, and it seemed as if they had been playing some sort of sex game.'

'The policeman on the spot was Larry Jensen.'

'Very handsome? That one? He wanted rid of me. I wonder why?'

'I got a call from the *Mircester Telegraph* this afternoon,' said Bill. 'They asked what this was all about – sex games at a village vicarage with a bishop taking part. I asked where he was getting this from and all he said was, "Tell Larry to phone me. Bert Finnegan, news desk."'

'So, I went in search of Larry to give him a rocket for leaking stories to the press and he wasn't home. He was supposed to be on duty today.'

'He was first on the scene when I phoned for help,' said Agatha.

'And what else?'

'Julian, the lawyer, invited us to his garden next door for drinks and we went there. One of the twins – it's hard to tell one from the other – was babbling on about bondage games. If Larry was selling stuff to the newspapers, he might feel he had hit gold. He may be there now looking for more dirt.'

Agatha's cats, Hodge and Boswell, had climbed up onto Bill's lap. 'My cats show more affection for you than they ever do for me,' said Agatha. 'Now, what?' For Charles had just strolled into the garden.

'What's up?' he asked. 'I saw the police car. I thought you tecs were supposed to drive around in un-marked cars.'

'Sometimes we do and sometimes we don't,' said Bill, made lazy by the warm, close air of the evening.

The phone rang and before Agatha could move, Charles had leapt to his feet to answer it. 'He's forgotten about the extension in the kitchen,' Agatha said. She darted into the kitchen, and seized the phone in time to hear Charles say primly, 'I am afraid Mrs Raisin is not at home.'

'Oh, yes she is,' howled Agatha. Bill heard her then say, 'Why, my very dear bishop, that would be lovely. I'll meet you there at eight.'

'Mistake,' said Charles when Agatha walked back into the garden.

'Jealous, Charles?'

'No, I am convinced he was the inventor of those sex games and I am sure he encouraged Helen into that business of punishing her husband.'

'Get this. I am being *paid* to investigate that missing heiress.'

'By Julian.'

'How did you guess?'

'Who else? Peter is not going to part with any cash. Oh, there goes the doorbell. I'll get it.'

'No, you don't,' said Agatha. 'My house, my doorbell.'

But when she opened the door and found Mavis and Millicent on the step, mirror images of outrage, she wished she *had* let Charles answer it.

'You are a scarlet woman!' howled Millicent.

'Nobody has said things like that since Victorian theatrical productions,' said Agatha. 'Say what you have to say and shove off. Scarlet woman, indeed, when you two pussies were playing bondage games. *Help!*'

For before she could leap back, Millicent had raked her nails down Agatha's cheek.

Agatha was lifted aside by Bill Wong. He got as far as, 'Millicent Dupin, I am arresting you on a charge of . . .' when Agatha said, 'I am not bringing charges.'

'Why not?' said Bill. Millicent began to sob. 'I feel sorry for them,' said Agatha, not in any Christian spirit of forgiveness but bearing out the wise words of Oscar Wilde, 'Forgive your enemies. There is nothing they hate more.'

This showed a shift in Agatha's inferiority complex, which recently would have suggested to her that people like the Dupins must have sniffed out her common background. The old Agatha would have thirsted for revenge.

'Run along,' said Agatha. 'Shoo!'

As the twins scampered into their old Daimler, Bill said, 'I wonder if you should get a tetanus shot.'

'I'll be all right.' Agatha peered at her face in the hall mirror. 'What a sodding mess. I should have charged her. I'm telling you, Bill, you can start looking for the Larry copper's body.'

She walked to the garden and Bill hurried after her. There were cries of dismay from Alice and Charles at the scratches on her face. 'No, tell them later,' said Bill. 'Why do you think we should be looking for Larry Jensen's dead body?'

'Oh, joke in bad taste, although I am beginning to think their infatuation is driving them mad. But when one of the twins, I forget which, started babbling about bondage when we found Peregrine with his head bashed, Larry had a nasty gleam in his eye.'

'We suspect him of selling stories to the newspapers,' said Alice. 'Oh, I am sure he'll turn up. Always hanging around.'

'Always hanging around you,' complained Bill.

Alice laughed. 'Hasn't a hope in hell.'

Agatha experienced a sharp pang of jealousy. Bill had been her very first friend in the Cotswolds, and, although he was at least thirty years younger than she was, Agatha wanted to be absolutely the only woman in her male friends' lives.

'If you've a first-aid kit,' said Alice, 'you had better let me fix your face for you. I gather one of the horrible twins did that. Why?'

'The besotted twosome were supposed to have dinner with the bishop tonight but he cancelled and they must have found out that the reason for the cancellation is because he is taking me out for dinner instead. The medicine box is under the sink.'

When they had gone upstairs to the bathroom, Bill laughed and said, 'That's our Aggie. She thinks we should be looking for Larry's dead body.'

'Maybe you should.' Said Charles.

* * *

The bell ringers finished their practice that evening and gathered round a table tombstone afterwards to sample the contents of a hamper sent to the Dupins by the bishop. Harry Bury and Gloria had complained about the heat and suggested they move outside to the graveyard. 'It do be an odd summer,' said Harry. 'Getting hotter and hotter.'

'I do not believe our dear bishop should cancel dinner with us to entertain that trollop,' complained Mavis, 'although it was sweet of him to send this hamper.'

'She's sexy,' said Colin Docherty, cracking his knuckles.

'Our dear bishop has a mind above such things,' said Millicent.

'Yes, but you precious pair ain't,' leered Harry.

The sisters half rose to stalk off but the humid heat made them sink down again. For once the bell ringers stopped quarrelling. It was just too hot and, even though the sun was going down, there seemed to be no relief.

The usually accurate weather forecast on television had been wrong. Thunderstorms were expected that evening, bringing in cooler air, and so Agatha had put aside the floaty silk chiffon dress she had planned to wear and had settled on a long royal blue velvet skirt with a matching jacket over a white satin blouse.

Her car was air-conditioned, but the steak house was not, and Agatha could almost feel her makeup beginning to melt. The bishop looked cool in a sky-blue linen shirt and matching trousers. Agatha was surprised. She had assumed he wore his bishop's purple on every occasion. For although there were many gorgeous robes for the different religious festivals, Peter Salver-Hinkley did seem overfond of purple. Certainly, it suited his classical features.

They conversed amiably about the weather. After they had ordered their steaks – Agatha's well-done and the bishop's extremely rare – he surprised her by saying he had just been grilled by the police.

'Oh, your missing heiress,' said Agatha. 'Has that come up again?'

For a moment, there was a stillness in him and a flash of something unlovely in his eyes, but it was gone in a moment and he said lightly, 'They are looking for some missing policeman.'

'They asked me about him earlier today,' said Agatha. 'Seems he had a nasty habit of selling stories to the newspapers and bondage games at a vicarage makes saucy reading.'

'I despise people like that,' said Peter. 'In fact, I don't know how you can bear your job.'

This gave Agatha an opportunity to brag about a former case and how clever she had been, and it was only when she had finished a long anecdote that she realised he had drunk most of the bottle of Merlot he had ordered and did not seem to be listening to her at all.

'It was nice of you to invite me out for dinner,' said Agatha. 'May I have some wine, please? Thank you. Can you see those claw marks on my face? I can feel my concealer melting in this heat. That was your precious Dupins, mad with rage because you cancelled dinner.'

'Oh, dear. I have been turning on the charm too much. The fact is when it comes to raising money for Help the Old, I am apt to be ruthless. We have an old folks' home and we hope to expand.' He suddenly smiled into Agatha's eyes and exuded such a wave of sexuality that Agatha actually blushed.

'Of course,' he said huskily, reaching across the table and running a thumb across the back of her hand, 'if you could find a way . . .'

Agatha withdrew her hand and said stiffly, 'I'll consult my accountant tomorrow and see what I can afford.'

'Good,' he said briskly, turning off that strong musky sexuality like someone turning off a tap. Poor Dupins, thought Agatha. Must be like being hit with a sledgehammer.

Neither had ordered a starter and their steaks arrived. Agatha began to feel slightly nauseated. Her steak seemed so large. Across the table, Peter was deftly slicing the bloodiest steak Agatha had ever seen. Behind her a couple with ya-ya voices were having something flambéed and the resultant wave of heat struck Agatha in the back of the neck.

But Julian was paying her to find out about the heiress, so Agatha said, 'Don't you often wonder what happened to Jennifer Toynby? After all, she was your fiancée.'

He carefully sliced off another slice of meat, letting a

small rivulet of blood run across his plate to form a blood lake amongst the vegetables.

He chewed slowly and carefully and then said in measured tones, 'My engagement had been long over. I gather she had discovered drugs. She will turn up one day in a rehab or a commune. Now, please let us talk about something else. I gather they are excavating the crypt at Thirk Magna.'

'Why?'

'We found some old documents which showed that the tomb of Sir Randolph Quentin, one of the Knights Templar, is buried there. They excavated a grave and have taken the bones away for DNA testing. When they are finished, the bones are returned and I give old Sir Quentin a Christian burial.'

Agatha wondered if she were suffering from something called prickly heat that she had only read about in books about the tropics. She desperately wanted to scratch her armpits. She stood up abruptly.

'Where are you going?' asked Peter.

'Where do you think?' demanded Agatha crossly.

The ladies' room was empty. She bathed her face and armpits in cold water and then carefully reapplied makeup. She wished she could just walk out the door and go home.

A woman walked in. She was wearing black trousers that looked as if they had been painted on her long stick-like legs. Over them, she wore a red chiffon blouse, semi-transparent, showing two pendulous sagging breasts. She had thick, black, lifeless hair and a haggard face.

'Your fellow's a real dreamboat,' she said to Agatha.

'He's not my fellow,' said Agatha. She suddenly wanted to walk away from the bishop with his bloody steak and that suffocating sexuality that he could turn on at will.

'I wonder,' said Agatha, 'if you would do me a favour and tell him I am not feeling very well and have gone home.'

'Delighted, I'm sure,' said her companion. 'Love a chance to talk to him.'

Agatha went out into the close, humid night. To her relief, a cab was cruising past and she hailed it.

It was only when she was home and sitting out in the garden with a cold gin and tonic in her hand that she wondered what had come over her. She was being paid to investigate. Not to run away. With some reluctance, she admitted to herself that Peter Salver-Hinkley frightened her.

Chapter Four

The next day, after Julian had signed a contract, Agatha decided to let her young assistants, Toni Gilmour and Simon Black, make a start on the case of the missing heiress. The weather was still suffocating. Black clouds had piled up in the sky and everyone had eagerly awaited a refreshing thunderstorm, but nothing had happened and, once again, a sun like polished brass shone down on the wilting population of the Cotswolds. People wore the minimum, and men who should never have gone bare-chested stripped off to expose shark's belly-white skin.

Agatha received a call from Mrs Bloxby to say that the crusader's bones were being returned to their grave in the crypt at Thirk Magna on the following day at five in the afternoon and would Agatha like to go to the ceremony. Agatha said she would not, but, after she had rung off, she told Toni and Simon about it and suggested they start their observation of the bishop there.

By the following afternoon, Agatha was beginning to feel like a wimp. The heat in that steak house had made her fancy things, that was all. She phoned Mrs Bloxby and said she would pick her up and that they would go to the ceremony together.

Agatha was wearing what she privately damned as her 'frump' clothes. This consisted of a loose blue linen housedress, bare legs and flat sandals. Mrs Bloxby, getting into Agatha's car, said, 'I see neither Sir Charles nor Mr Lacey will be joining us?'

'See?' demanded Agatha. 'Odd way of putting it. I expect to see one of them holding up a sign which says, WE'RE NOT GOING.'

And *you* should be holding a sign saying, NO ONE WORTH DRESSING UP FOR IS GOING TO BE THERE, thought Mrs Bloxby. Whereas I am wearing my best cotton shirtwaister because I am a saint. As the car moved off, Mrs Bloxby giggled.

'What's the joke?' asked Agatha.

'Just the heat getting to me,' said the vicar's wife, who did not want to explain that she found her bout of saintliness absolutely ridiculous. Yet, she thought wistfully, we vicars' wives have so little to feel superior about.

'I am not looking forward to meeting Helen Toms again,' said Agatha. 'She's the sort of woman Scotland Yard calls a "murderee". You know. The perpetual victim.'

'That is a bit harsh,' said Mrs Bloxby. 'Our dear bishop has caused a lot of upset here and there. Now, Alf told me last night that Peregrine Toms had found God.'

'Sounds like a parcel. Had he lost Him?'

'Obviously. Wife beating and gentle Jesus meek and mild don't quite go together. He is to preach a sermon

61

in the church just before the bishop arrives for the rebur-ial ceremony.'

'You might have told me,' complained Agatha. 'I thought that in five minutes' time I would be standing on the vicarage lawn with a ciggie in one hand and a drink in the other. Now I learn I am to be cooped up in a hot-as-hell church listening to some bore.'

'Mrs Raisin, I must explain . . .'

'Oh, for God's sake,' said Agatha, stopping outside the vicarage by slamming on the brakes. 'My name is Agatha, get it? All this second name malarkey is begin-ning to sound camp.'

Mrs Bloxby got out of the car and walked towards the church without looking around. Agatha stared mutin-ously through the windscreen and then lit a cigarette. She did not care if she had offended her best friend. Screw everybody.

She had the engine running to keep the air-conditioning on. Suddenly she saw Mrs Bloxby, her face paper-white, being supported from the church by the sexton, Harry Bury.

Agatha switched off the engine and hurtled from the car. 'I'm sorry,' she shouted.

'Get her a cup of tea,' said Harry, 'and look after her. I've got to go. Ringing a peal for the bishop.'

Agatha put an arm around her friend's shoulders and led her to a flat tombstone. 'What happened?'

'I had just got inside the church,' said Mrs Bloxby, 'when a fat fly landed on my face. I smacked it against my cheek and then looked at my hand and it was covered in blood. It had probably been feeding off some dead animal's carcass. I realise that now, but I was suddenly sure there was a dead body in the church.'

'Only bones,' said Agatha. 'Oh, damn it to hell. The bells have started.'

They both looked up at the square Norman tower. Above the tower, the black clouds had returned and were piling up against the sky. Agatha sat with her arm still around her friend's thin shoulders.

'I shouldn't have been so rude to you,' said Agatha. 'It's the heat and this place. Oh, hello, Toni.'

'I thought you weren't going to come,' said Toni. 'Here's Simon as well. Mrs Bloxby! Has something happened? You look so white. I'll get you a glass of water.'

Toni ran off through the churchyard. She was wearing sky-blue shorts and a blue chiffon blouse. She came back and handed Mrs Bloxby a glass of water.

'A fly landed on my face,' said the vicar's wife. 'I smacked it and my hand came away covered in blood.'

The sound of the tenor bell summoned them to church. The old Norman church did not have a very attractive interior. Cromwell's men had shattered all the stained glass so the windows were all made of plain glass. The saints had been wrenched from their plinths. The only thing of any beauty was a wooden altar painted in gold and green, an exquisite thing.

The congregation shuffled in. Then came the high voice of one of the Dupins – Agatha was not sure which one as the twins sounded alike – 'I wish some people would *realise* the *importance* of washing in hot weather.'

The air was full of the noisy buzzing of flies. And that sweetish, cloying smell!

The bishop and the dean arrived, Peter having forsaken his favourite purple for leaf green.

Everyone began to shift uncomfortably in the hard pews as Peregrine began to rant. He said that digging up the crusader was blasphemy and God would punish them all. Agatha was just beginning to wonder if he would ever shut up when Peter rose and simply elbowed Peregrine aside, whispering savagely, 'Go and put your head in a bucket of cold water.'

Peter smiled down on the small congregation. The Dupin sisters clasped their hands and silently worshipped at the altar of his manly beauty.

'We are gathered together . . .' began Peter, but that was as far as he got.

'Death!' shouted a farmer seated in a back pew. 'That's what that there smell is and it's coming from the crypt.'

'He's right,' said Agatha in a loud voice. 'I've smelt death before.'

Peter looked round the congregation and his eyes fell on the sexton. The bishop, Agatha was to learn, had a very good memory. 'Mr Bury, is it not? Well, I suggest, Mr Bury, if the organist would like to play something while you go and investigate, perhaps you can put their fears to rest.'

Peggy Comfort was a reporter with the *Mircester Telegraph.* She was twenty-one years old and determined to be a hard-hitting journalist. She was sure that her editor, Charlie Soames, had spotted her potential. She did not know that her generous bust and blonde hair gave the editor ideas of an altogether different and alluring potential. She slid quietly out of her pew and made her way down the stairs to the crypt. Harry Bury was lying unconscious beside the excavated grave of the crusader. In the yellowish overhead light, his face had a sinister bluish tinge.

Immediately, Peggy imagined herself on television, describing how she had saved his life. She bent over him and, in doing so, looked down into the grave and at the crawling, sickening mass of flies covering a body. Her scream was tremendous. It rose up from the crypt and sent the birds, roosting in the graveyard trees, up to the stormy sky. It was a scream such as Fay Wray gave in the original *King Kong*. Six miles away in Moreton-in-Marsh, people were to swear the next day that they had heard that terrible scream.

As the congregation was about to rush to the crypt, Peter called in a stentorian voice, 'I will go. My dean will accompany me. If we need more help, we will call.'

Fortunately, neither he nor the dean looked round or they would have seen Agatha, her two detectives and Mrs Bloxby following close behind.

Peggy had stopped screaming and was being sick in a corner. The dean Donald Whitby bent over the fly-covered corpse. 'I'll call an ambulance but I think he's dead. Can you make out what's under all those flies, Peter?'

'I'll wait for the police. Oh, let's get out of here and phone. That awful smell!'

Toni opened her handbag and took out a can of something called Fly Off and sprayed it into the grave. Heavy bloated flies rose up in a cloud and Agatha screamed as some lodged in her hair. She suddenly felt dizzy and faint and longed to escape the dreadful scene but did not want to show weakness in front of her detectives.

Toni and Simon then eased Harry Bury away from the grave. 'It's that missing policeman,' said Agatha, taking one last stomach-heaving look at the dead face exposed by Toni's Fly Off spray. 'It's Larry Jensen.'

'We can't just leave this sexton,' said Toni. 'Simon, I've got a defibrillator in my car. Here are my keys. Run and get it and I'll try the kiss of life.'

Never had Agatha admired her assistant more as Toni put her lips to the blue lips of the sexton. That was until she heard Mrs Bloxby murmur, 'That girl is a saint,' and was consumed by a flash of jealousy because the sick reporter was wiping her mouth on her skirt and taking out her camera.

A flash of lightning stabbed through a long window at the end of the crypt and lit up the tableau of Toni, her blonde hair spilling over Harry Bury's face. It was the photograph that was to go around the world and secure Peggy a job on a national newspaper. It earned her the nickname of Flash in the Pan because her subsequent reporting was very amateur. Toni cried, 'There's a pulse.'

Forgetting her jealousy in her excitement, Agatha

called to Simon who had come hurrying down the stairs. 'Hurry up! He isn't dead yet.'

As the ambulance men arrived, Harry was jerked back to life.

Agatha, Toni, Simon and Mrs Bloxby sat together in a pew near the entrance to the church as outside the storm yelled and shouted, throwing down sheets of rain, claps of thunder, and finally a great stab of lightning which split one of the old tombstones in half. It bore the legend, HERE LYETH JOHN SOMMER. COME AND GET ME IF YOU CAN, I BE SAFE FROM THE DEVIL, THAT I AM.

They had all given preliminary statements to the police. Agatha craved a cigarette but she had left them in her car. She heard Mrs Bloxby murmur, 'Very well done, Miss Gilmour,' and forced herself to say, 'That was very brave of you, Toni.'

'The rain's stopping,' said Toni. 'I feel a bit sick. The pub's open. I could murder a drink.'

'We'll all go,' said Agatha. 'Simon, go and tell one of those policemen where to find us. Anyone know what the pub is called?'

'It's called The Bells,' said Simon. 'Tiny place.'

'Lead the way,' said Agatha.

'Are you sure?' asked Mrs Bloxby. 'Press and television will be arriving soon.'

'I am like any other small business,' said Agatha. 'It pays to advertise.'

* * *

But before they reached the pub, they were waylaid by Bishop Peter. He smiled at Agatha and said, 'Won't you introduce me to your daughter?'

He immediately saw he had made a mistake by the frosty look in Agatha's eyes. He tried to backpedal by saying he had assumed such beauty came from a beautiful mother and who was more beautiful than Agatha Raisin?

Toni gave him a warm smile and said, 'Oh, do stop digging. You are in the muck deep enough. Come along, Agatha.' And as she walked away, her high clear voice carried back to the bishop as it was meant to do, 'The man must be blind. But that's dirty old men for you.'

'Now that was too harsh,' said Agatha.

'He frightens me and I don't know why,' said Toni.

Mrs Bloxby stopped outside the pub. 'I would like to go home,' she said. 'Perhaps Toni or Simon could drop me off. It isn't far.'

'I'll do it,' said Toni.

'I'd better,' said Simon. 'The press will want to interview Toni and I haven't told the police where we are yet.'

They found the pub served soup and sandwiches and decided to stay for lunch. Agatha gave interviews to the local press. She assured Simon afterwards that she was just about to describe Toni's courage when two reporters from the nationals walked in, one of them saying loudly, 'Where's this gorgeous life-saving blonde?'

Agatha was forgotten. Peggy had emailed her famous photo of Toni saving Harry to the *Daily News* who then sold it around the world. Simon had returned and was describing the scene in the crypt as the photographers arrived to join the reporters and soon were busy taking photographs.

Agatha was just about to suggest they leave when the pub door opened and a tall man slouched in. It transpired that he worked for the *Sun* because Agatha heard another reporter hail him with, 'How's things at the *Sun*?' He had been out of town on a story in Cheltenham when he had heard the news on the radio, he said. He paused in the doorway and looked across at Agatha. That was all it took. One long assessing look from eyes as green as grass and Agatha Raisin fell instantly and completely in love for the first time in her life. The others had been obsession. This was real.

She had never believed in love at first sight. Nor had she ever envisaged being struck down by it after one long look from a tall, thin reporter who bore a remarkable resemblance to Buster Keaton. The voices rose and fell about her ears. Toni gave interview after interview, always careful to mention Agatha and the agency. Agatha felt encased in a golden bubble of love.

Simon watched her out of the corner of his eye. He liked Charles and always assumed that he and Agatha would get married one day. Had she known the chap from the *Sun* before? But he was soon distracted by Toni's protests that she did not want to pose for any more photographs. Then Sky News and Midlands Television arrived. Toni looked to Agatha for help but that lady was staring into space with a dreamy look on her face.

Distraction came in the form of the Dupin sisters. Rattling collection tins and crying, 'Money for the Abbey's Old Folks' Home,' they circulated the pub.

Agatha rose to go and Simon felt relieved. She would never have walked out so calmly if she had been at all keen on the fellow.

'Do you want me to stay?' asked Simon.

'I don't think Toni will be allowed any freedom for a while so you're on your own, but try to find out when Larry was last seen around the village. He must have been trying to dig up some muck about the bondage games to flog to the press. He must have been killed, say, yesterday.'

'Why?'

'Flies,' said Agatha. 'The weather has been stinking hot since he disappeared. You'd think he'd have been crawling with maggots by now.'

'Wrong way round,' said Simon. 'Maggots turn into flies after about four to six days.'

'Whatever.' Agatha hated to be corrected. 'No, you are the one who is wrong. Flies lay eggs on the dead body. Okay? *They lay eggs*. Then eggs to larvae sometimes in as little as twenty-four hours. The maggots feed for about five days, *then* the pupa cases and *then* buzz, buzz, buzz. Like me. I'm buzzing off.'

'And what are you going to do?'

Go home and dream and wait, was what Agatha should have said if telling the truth. But instead she said,

'I am going to call on Mrs Bloxby. I think the trouble all started with Mrs Toms.'

It was only when she had reached the outskirts of Carsely that Agatha began to shiver with delayed shock. She sadly decided that one glorious glimpse of love had been a false defence against the horror she had just witnessed. So, she decided to make sure Mrs Bloxby was all right.

When the vicar's wife answered the door, she looked flustered and upset. 'I feel very selfish,' she said. 'Mrs Toms wanted me to go and comfort her and I just can't. Something about the police having found out she was possibly the last person to see that policeman before he was murdered. Oh, do come in. Sherry?'

'Yes, please.' Agatha slumped back against the old feather cushions on the sofa and stared at the flickering flames of the fire. Why had Mrs Bloxby lit a fire on a summer's day? The sun was shining through the window, bleaching the flames. Shock, decided Agatha. We are all cold with shock.

When Mrs Bloxby returned with two glasses of sherry and sat down beside Agatha, she said, 'There are times, you know, when one just has to be selfish. Now, if I believed that Mrs Toms was genuinely in need of help, of course I would have gone. But there was something in her voice that seemed to suggest she was enjoying the drama. How is Miss Gilmour? Perhaps we should not have left her.'

71

'Simon is with her. Oh, dear. That is not enough. I'll phone Patrick Mulligan to act as watchdog.'

Mrs Bloxby waited until she finished talking to Patrick. Then she said, 'I thought Sir Charles might have been there.'

Agatha shrugged. 'He comes and goes. It's all money with Charles, you know. Every time he disappears, it's because he is romancing some deb who has bags of money. Now, I am sure Roy Silver will arrive shortly.'

Roy, a public relations officer, was a former employee of Agatha's when she ran her own publicity business. Although his job was to get publicity for clients, he craved the limelight for himself and Agatha's past cases had meant that he had sometimes been filmed talking to the press.

Agatha tilted her glass and watched little rivulets of sherry running down the inside.

'Tell me, do you believe in love at first sight? Across a crowded room and all that jazz?'

Must have happened after I left, thought Mrs Bloxby. Aloud, she said, 'Of course. I saw Alf at the May Ball in Oxford and that was that.'

'So happily ever after?'

'Only in fairy stories. Real love comes along after a couple of years. You know, kindness, tolerance and caring.'

Goodness, that sounds boring, thought Agatha. Where's the pizazz?

'Was he in the pub?'

'Who?' asked Agatha.

'The man who started you thinking about love at first sight.'

Agatha's bearlike eyes studied the faded wallpaper, then the fire, and then she shrugged. 'I must go. I keep forgetting that Julian is paying me to find out what happened to the missing heiress. I may as well visit her parents.'

So, there is someone, thought Mrs Bloxby sadly. Poor Charles. But maybe Charles would not really care. Agatha was a rich woman but not rich enough for mercenary Charles.

Agatha's grandmother had come south from the highlands of Scotland to find work in one of the Birmingham factories. Perhaps Agatha had inherited her intuition. She had a sudden acute awareness that the reporter from the *Sun* was waiting outside her cottage. The strength of her feelings frightened her. To surrender to such a love would mean losing control.

Agatha got into her car outside the vicarage and looked up the address of Jennifer Toynby's parents. They lived in a house called The Beeches and it lay some miles out of Moreton-in-Marsh, just off the Fosseway.

The first star was appearing in the evening sky as she turned in at the gates of The Beeches and rolled along a short drive.

* * *

Charles got out of his car in front of Agatha's cottage. A tall, slim man was leaning on the gate.

'What are you doing here?' demanded Charles.

'Reporter, *Sun*, Terry Fletcher,' he said laconically. 'You?'

'Charles Fraith. Why are you here?'

'To get her reaction.'

'To what?'

'Where have you been? To get her reaction to finding a dead body in the crypt of the church in Thirk Magna.'

'First I've heard of it,' said Charles. He walked up to the door and put a key in the lock and let himself in. Terry watched him go in. Then he went to his own car, got in and drove off.

The Beeches was built from red brick, more like the houses of Warwickshire than the mellow golden stone ones of the Cotswolds.

Despite the warmth of the evening, Agatha felt cold and wished she had brought a cardigan or jacket. Her reaction to that reporter, she decided again, had been caused by shock.

She rang the bell. A thin woman in denim overalls answered the door. 'You vant?' she asked. From the height of her cheekbones and the mid-European accent, Agatha guessed she was the maid.

'Mr or Mrs Toynby at home?'

'Vich wan you want?'

'Either?'

'Vat?'

The maid leaned against the doorpost, took a cigarette packet out of her pocket, fished out a cigarette, lit it, took a puff and smiled at Agatha.

Agatha took out one of her cards. 'Please tell the Toynbys I wish to speak to them. *And do it now!*'

'Gerda!' came a sharp voice. 'Who is it?'

The maid flicked her cigarette out into the drive and turned and handed Agatha's card to, who Agatha supposed, was Mrs Toynby.

'I can't read this,' she complained. 'Come into the drawing room.'

She led the way into one of those peculiarly soulless rooms, the result of a professional interior decorator. The main colour themes were green and brown.

'Oh, you are one of those!' cried Mrs Toynby. 'She's one of those, Arthur.'

A head peered over the back of a green silk-covered armchair. 'Hooker?'

'Don't be silly. She's a detective.'

'I'm not being silly. Gerda lets everyone in these days. Do you remember—'

His wife interrupted harshly. 'I haven't any time for you,' she said to Agatha. 'We hired detectives when our poor baby disappeared. Waste of space.'

She was a small woman with lank brown hair high-lighted with violet streaks. Her round face was covered in thick makeup and her thin lips were painted bright orange. All in all, she looked like a badly painted sunset.

Wonder how they made their money, thought Agatha.

75

They're not posh. Pair of pseuds. Should have looked that up instead of dreaming of love striking across a crowded room and all that jazz. I am a disgrace to feminism. I don't care. I want to end my days in the arms of some man.

Aloud she said, 'Someone has hired me to look into the disappearance of your daughter.'

'You don't expect us to pay anything?'

'Not a penny.'

'Oh, do come and sit down. Turn your chair around, Arthur. Someone else is paying her to find our baby.'

Arthur, who had been staring out of the window, walked his chair around because it was on castors. He was wearing a cravat and a sports jacket tailored in the noisiest tweed Agatha had ever seen.

Mrs Toynby sat in another armchair after placing an upright chair facing her and it was into this chair she urged Agatha to sit. Then she yelled, 'Gerda!'

The maid slouched in. 'We'll have coffee, Gerda.'

'Evening off, missus.'

'Oh, push off then. We'll have drinks instead. You can't have any, Raisin woman, because you are driving. Get me a large Scotch, Arthur.'

'Get it yourself, you lazy bitch.'

'How dare you talk to me like that? HOW DARE YOU? I'll fix you. You'll see.'

Mrs Toynby went to a trolley at the side of the room that contained an assortment of bottles. She poured a full glass of whisky, carried it to her husband and poured it over his head. He spluttered, dried his eyes, jumped to his feet and hit his wife on the nose.

She screamed in pain as Agatha rose and quietly retreated to the hall where she phoned the police and reported a 'domestic'. Then she retreated to her car and lit up a cigarette.

It was half an hour before a police car rolled up. 'It's not my fault if he's killed her,' complained Agatha. 'What kept you?'

'A real murder,' said one. 'Village where a body was found in the crypt.'

'Oh, that. I was there,' said Agatha. 'I've given my statement so get in there and stop that war.'

Agatha returned home, feeling weary. Neither of the Toynbys was prepared to charge the other, and, as no bones had been broken, the police had left them to it.

Charles was sleeping on the sofa, the cats sprawled on top of him.

Agatha poured herself a gin and tonic and switched on her laptop to look up the Toynbys. Probably made their money from lavatory seats or something really awful, thought Agatha.

But it transpired the Toynbys' grandparents had not only been of the landed gentry but had made a fortune buying up villagers' cottages because they saw that one day most people would own a car and cars meant trips to the picturesque Cotswolds and a desire to retire there.

Last week, one of their 'bijou' cottages had sold for half a million pounds.

The difficulty of finding out anything about Jennifer, thought Agatha, was that her parents were so weird, she doubted if she could get a sensible word out of either of them. Now, Peter, the bishop, he has to know something.

Surely her home life must have been a misery if Ma and Pa spent their days assaulting each other. But Bishop Peter might talk to, say, Charles. She woke him up. The cats slid onto the floor, looking up at her sulkily.

'Where have you been?' asked Charles.

Agatha swung his legs onto the floor and sat down next to him on the sofa. She told him about the Toynbys and then suggested he tackle the bishop about Jennifer's home life. Afterwards, Charles was to blame himself for turning her down.

'Stop using me as an unpaid detective,' he said.

Agatha was tired and disappointed. Love at first sight had not happened. Most of the press knew where she lived and he hadn't been waiting for her, that reporter with the green eyes. There was just Charles in her life now, who came and went just as he pleased.

Well, no longer! 'Charles, I want my keys back. In other words, I want my privacy back. I don't want you wandering in and out when you feel like it.'

Agatha had demanded her keys back several times before. Charles usually just found a way of getting them copied.

'I'll come back when you're in a better mood.' Agatha heard the front door close and for the first time in her life she knew what it was to be completely alone. She had felt lonely before, but it had always been a fleeting feeling. Now, though, it was as if the long years of life to come, entirely on her own, had entered into her mind and body and wouldn't go away.

The cats tried to climb onto her lap but she shoved them away. 'You always prefer someone else,' she shouted. 'Sod off or tomorrow the pair of you are fur slippers.'

She hugged herself and shivered. I am going bonkers, she thought, and all because of some fantasy about a man with green eyes. My poor cats. I've got a bit of lamb's liver. I'll cook it up for them.

She was walking towards the kitchen when the doorbell rang: sharp, shrill and imperative. Agatha slowly opened the door.

A pair of green eyes looked down into her own. 'I'm Terry Fletcher, reporter for the *Sun*, and you are Agatha Raisin. Now do we faff about? Or do we go to bed?'

Charles drove back to Agatha's cottage. He realised now that she had looked unusually sad. He would offer to see the bishop for her. As he got out of his car, he noticed another car parked in front of the house with a press sticker in the window. The curtains in Agatha's sitting room were not quite drawn closed. Something prompted him to go quietly up to the window and look inside. What he saw made him slowly back away.

He went to James Lacey's house next door and rang the bell.

'What is it?' demanded James when he opened the door. 'I was just about to go to bed.'

'It's Agatha.'

'Oh, come in. What has the wretched woman done now?'

'She's fallen in love.'

'Well, she used to be in love with me,' said James, 'and yet now she is totally indifferent to my charms. Charles, she's been in and out of love several times.'

Charles followed James into his sitting room and hunched down on the sofa. 'I looked through the curtains. They weren't at it. They were just standing there, gazing rapturously into each other's eyes. The full Tristan and Isolde bit. She's radiant.'

'I'll get you a brandy. It won't last. Agatha instinctively goes for flawed men.'

'Like you?'

'Yes, I suppose like me. After we were married, I wanted her to behave like a little housewife. You could have married her yourself, Charles. Here's your brandy.'

'We did sort of discuss it one time. It wouldn't work. Can you imagine Agatha opening fêtes and things?'

'Your aunt does that and could go on doing it.'

'My man, Gustav, can't stand her.'

'If you loved her, it wouldn't matter what Gustav thought.'

'She wants me to find out more about Bishop Peter and the missing heiress,' said Charles. 'I'll get on with that.'

'Who is this lover boy?'

'Some reporter. Got a press sticker on his car.'

'Young?'

'No, about Agatha's age.'

'Then he's married. They always are, you know. Wife tucked away in Orpington or somewhere like that while they are up in London having an affair with a nurse. Just be around to pick up the pieces.'

It was like living inside a bottle of champagne, thought Agatha during the next few days, as she felt herself sparkle and fizz. Terry went off to find out if there was anything to report and Agatha just stayed in her cottage and waited for his return. She had put Toni in charge of the office, saying that she was unwell. Terry was Australian. He said he would take her back with him in a few weeks' time to meet his family. To Agatha, it was as if the pair of them had become one person. No more loneliness. No more feeling less than.

Terry had said that he had to go to London for a few hours but that he would be back by the evening. Agatha dimly felt she should use the time until his return by doing a little detecting. But she soon gave up the idea to indulge in that glorious feeling of waiting and waiting for the moment the lover walks through the door.

The doorbell rang at four in the afternoon. Agatha scowled. She wanted to be left alone with this glorious feeling of anticipation. It rang again, shrill and peremptory.

Then she felt a surge of pure gladness. It must be Terry, back earlier than he had thought he would be.

Agatha opened the door. A small woman with blonde hair stood on the step. 'May I come in?'

'Who are you?' demanded Agatha.

'I'm Terry's wife.'

'Come in,' said Agatha, thinking rapidly, I didn't know he was married. He must have asked for a divorce.

She led the way into the sitting room. Mrs Fletcher took off her coat. Agatha blinked and then felt as if she had been dropped down a lift shaft because Mrs Fletcher was about seventh months pregnant. Through lips that appeared to have become cold and numb, Agatha said, 'You are expecting a child?'

'Yes, it'll be our fifth.'

'And why are you here?'

'One of the journalists on this story phoned me and told me what was going on.'

Agatha sat down suddenly. She wanted to cry. There was a great hard lump in her throat. Finally, she said in a choked voice, 'Has this happened before?'

'Oh, every time I get pregnant.'

'And you forgive him and go and see the other woman?'

'He usually talks to them himself. But in this case, he refused. He said he was taking you to Australia and then he would file for divorce. I've never seen him this bad.'

Agatha sat very quietly, her hands in her lap, mentally looking down at the wreck of the most wonderful thing that had ever happened to her. But he had lied by omission. If he had said he was married, she would never have had an affair with him.

'Would you like something to drink?' she offered. 'Don't worry. I won't see him again.'

'I would like you to phone for a taxi for me.'

'I'll drive you to the station.'

'No, Mrs Raisin, I think you will appreciate the fact that I never want to see you again.'

So, Agatha phoned and they both sat and waited in silence for what felt to Agatha like a month but was in fact only ten minutes.

When Mrs Fletcher had gone, Agatha packed a suit-case with cold and stiff fingers. She dropped her cats off with her cleaner, Doris Simpson, and then drove to the George Hotel in Mircester and checked in.

As she unpacked, she wondered that such glory, such *rightness* should all turn out to be fool's gold. One day she would cry, but not yet.

She ate a solitary dinner at the George that evening. Agatha decided she would never go near that cursed village of Thirk Magna again. Some evil must haunt that place. But it was time she got back to work. She was being paid to find out about the missing heiress. That visit to the parents had been a waste of time. She should have waited until they had finished shouting at each other and asked about Jennifer's friends.

83

Agatha sensed she was being stared at and turned round. Bishop Peter Salver-Hinkley was entertaining a couple of elderly ladies. They must be very rich, thought Agatha, to justify a visit to the George.

Peter saw her, said something to his companions and walked across the restaurant.

He must have a hide like a rhinoceros, thought Agatha. He must know by now that I do not like him. Still, he seems hell bent on getting money for that old folks' home so he can't be all bad.

'Beautiful as ever,' said Peter, pulling out a chair and sitting down next to her. 'But wounded! I can see it in your eyes.'

'Stop talking rubbish,' snapped Agatha. 'I am being hired to find out what happened to Jennifer. Any ideas?'

'Yes.' He got to his feet. 'Mind your own business. Things could get nasty.'

'Are you threatening me?' demanded Agatha in a loud voice.

The diners stared. He coloured and leaned over her. 'Use your brains for once in your life, dear lady.'

Now, that was interesting, thought Agatha. Unless he is guilty about something, there was no need for him to threaten me. All he had to do was say he hadn't the faintest idea.

But a wave of misery crashed over her as she thought of Terry. He should have told her he was married. Oh, God, it had seemed so right. It had seemed like everything the poets had written about and every pop song had a special meaning. She suddenly thought of Charles.

She should not have sent him away. He would be some sort of comfort.

At that moment, Charles felt he was in need of comfort. His valet-cum-butler-cum-general-servant, Gustav, packed up the account books. 'Don't you keep all that written stuff on a computer?' said Charles.

'Both,' said Gustav. 'This way and also on the computer. You are in the red and badly so, sir. I am afraid that you might need to marry Penelope Worth.'

'What makes you think she'll have me?'

'She'll have anyone. Ugly as sin, sir. Face like a cow's arse.'

After Gustav had left, Charles suddenly decided to talk it over with Agatha. He travelled to Carsely and coaxed from the cleaner the news that Agatha could be found at the George.

He found Agatha brooding over a black coffee. She stared at him in silence. Oh, dear, thought Charles, looking into Agatha's small bearlike eyes. I could kill the bastard. Do I ask about it? No. Bad idea.

'I need your help, Aggie,' he said, sitting down next to her. 'I need money. No, I am not asking you for any. But have you any ideas?'

'Sell land for building. Make a mint.'

'Can't sell agricultural land. Gustav says marriage is the only answer. Marriage to some fright.'

'Don't!' said Agatha harshly.

'Don't what?'

'Don't damn some woman because of her appearance. God, I am sick of men.'

Agatha signalled to the waiter. 'Double brandy,' she ordered.

'And one for me and a coffee,' said Charles.

'For which you will pay?'

'I will pay your whole bill, my angel, if you can think up a scheme to get me out of the red.'

'What about the ghost tours? Why did you stop those?'

'Some local reporter exposed all the special effects.'

'I see you are clutching a laptop, Charles. Let's see the worst.'

They drank brandy and coffee. Agatha automatically ordered more. 'Ah, you've been fiddling around with lousy stocks. You used to have a good man. What happened?'

'Fellow at the club said Forsyth & Williams were making a mint for him.'

'So, you gave them carte blanche.'

'Don't rub it in.'

'And they were still thinking the dot-com industry was the way to El Dorado. We'll go up to the City tomorrow and switch things over to my man. Then we'll get you some sort of bridge loan until you start earning again. But you have to do some work for me. I don't understand people like Jennifer's parents. I have a feeling you could winkle stuff out of them. Deal?'

'Deal. Uh-oh! Here comes trouble.'

Agatha did not turn round but she knew it was Terry.

'I must speak to you,' he said urgently.

'Go away,' said Agatha in a thin voice. 'Go home. Look after your wife. Never speak to me or approach me again.'

'Please, don't mind me,' said Charles.

'Agatha, I'll get a divorce.'

'Oh, please go away,' said Agatha wearily. 'Your duty lies with your children. Shove off.'

'May I be of help?' The three stared in amazement at Bishop Peter who was beaming on the group with an avuncular smile although his eyes were filled with avid curiosity. This Raisin woman must be a hotshot between the sheets.

Charles looked at him in simple amazement. 'Peter, you not only take the biscuit but the whole packet of shortbread. Do you usually butt in?'

'When I can see that my pastoral skills may be needed.'

Agatha stared at him. 'I think you're stark-raving bonkers. I'm going to bed. You are all bonkers.' Terry grabbed her arm as she stood up. Enraged with lost love, Agatha punched him full on the nose and then burst into tears.

Charles hustled her out of the dining room and into the lift. 'Don't speak,' he said. 'Here's a hankie. I don't want to know.'

'You're damn well not sleeping with me.'

'That is exactly what I am going to do, and I mean sleeping. We can then shove off to London in the morning.'

The first thing Agatha did was go into the bathroom, undress and have a shower where her salty tears mingled with the water, wondering all the while how a love that had seemed so perfect and golden had turned out to be so rubbish.

Charles joined her in bed afterwards, but only mumbling a good night and then falling asleep.

It was too late for a bigger piece to appear the next day in the *Mircester Telegraph* but there was a short paragraph to say that a reporter, Terence Fletcher, had been arrested for assaulting the bishop of Mircester. The day was grey and humid, suiting Agatha's mood of numb misery.

She wondered occasionally who had murdered that policeman. Funny how she and everyone else had not really worried about it. He had been killed by a hammer blow, or something like a hammer, to the head. But let the police worry about it. No one was paying her to find out about Larry.

After dealing, she thought, efficiently with Charles's financial problems, Agatha reminded him of his promise to try to get something out of the Toynby parents. Just so long as she kept away from Thirk Magna and concentrated on the missing heiress, then she would feel she could heal and get over the loss of love.

She did not know that tempers were rising in Thirk Magna, and all fury was directed at Millicent Dupin.

Chapter Five

The annual village fête was to be held in Thirk Magna on the fifth of June as usual. A special peal of bells was to be rung, a peal with a difference. For it had been mathematically constructed by schoolteacher, Colin Docherty. As the peal was only an hour long and not a marathon, the others amiably agreed. That was until Gloria started 'stepping out' with a 'gentleman friend' who said the peal was rubbish. This paragon, she said, had been at the rehearsal.

The weather continued hot, sunless, close and humid. The Dupin sisters began to see cracks in Colin's programme. They had always rung the Thirk Triples and tradition surely must count for something. Helen Toms said that something new was nice and Julian agreed. But the others were swinging back to tradition and Colin was shouting and yelling when Bishop Peter made a surprise appearance.

He said he would talk to the sisters alone.

They retreated to the drawing room. The sexton, Harry Bury, fully recovered, rounded on Colin. 'Couldn't you just have left it alone?'

He was backed by the butcher, Joseph Merrydown.

At last the sisters and the bishop reappeared. For the sake of peace and quiet, Millicent explained, they were going to revert to tradition and play Colin's ring on the following Sunday. Colin stamped off in a rage. Julian ran after him. The Dupin twins beamed all round and proudly announced that they would be ringing the bells *in armour* and would be photographed in all the locals and Midlands television as well.

The bishop's collection of armour was famous. They were all invited the following day to the palace to get fitted out.

'It'll be very hot,' said Helen Toms.

'Thought about that,' said the butcher. 'We'll put them on for the photos but not the actual ringing.' They were all seduced into friendly behaviour by the thought of the joys of dressing up and getting their photographs in the local newspapers.

The following day, Mrs Bloxby was trying to persuade Agatha to join her at the celebrations in Thirk Magna. 'The press have all gone apart from the locals,' said the vicar's wife. 'I did promise Mrs Toms I would go. It is on a Saturday, after all, and you have stopped working on Saturdays. I am truly sorry about your affair but life must go on.'

Agatha heaved a sigh. She began to wish she had never told her friend about the affair. She did not want to confess that she was actually considering hunting

Terry down and saying that she would go to Australia with him. They could send money to make sure the children had every comfort.

But he would not be there and Julian was beginning to demand some sort of results. Charles seemed to have disappeared so she did not know if he had found anything out. Agatha suddenly wished she could just get in her car and keep on driving and driving, away from her memories of golden love, away from duty and work, driving until she was exhausted and couldn't think anymore.

Mrs Bloxby silently prayed, 'Oh, dear God, send her another man,' and then blushed at what she thought must be the most idiotic prayer she had ever uttered.

'All right. I'll go with you,' said Agatha. 'But you mustn't let Helen Toms take up so much of your time. She is a professional martyr.'

That maybe makes two of us, thought Agatha miserably. Why am I still longing for a cheat and a liar?

It certainly was not suitable weather to wear armour and ring bells while wearing it. But this was glory for the bell ringers of Thirk Magna as local press and television photographed the grotesque sight of eight bell ringers in full armour. But the demonstration only lasted ten minutes because Helen Toms fainted and fell with a crash to the floor of the bell chamber. Mavis raised her visor, her face contorted with rage, a rage fuelled by the sight of the bishop and Julian Brody bending over Helen.

Only when Mavis and the others realised that a television crew was recording every angry syllable did they begin to behave themselves. Agatha, one of the small audience who had managed to get a place in the chamber, felt weak with laughter, almost cleansed of the episode with Terry.

Colin perhaps was the angriest of all because it was his changes that should have been chosen. Helen was led away by her husband who had been summoned to help. Mavis said she could handle both sallies and seized Helen's abandoned rope. Outside, the villagers set up a ragged cheer as the noisy – cacophony to the uninitiated, music of God to any campanologist – started up again. The bell ringers had silently agreed to keep the armour on, seduced by the idea of watching themselves on television.

Agatha and Mrs Bloxby strolled round the fête afterwards. Usual stands. Bring and Buy. Tombola. Secondhand books, one small pile to be signed by a local author whom most people snubbed to show they were not impressed in the slightest. Skittles, hamburger stand, swings and roundabouts, all the fun of the fair.

Bishop Peter and his dean, Donald Whitby, were passing out fliers for the abbey's old folks' home. Agatha raised her eyes at the prices. A month's stay cost nearly seven thousand pounds. And that was only for the basics. How many relatives visiting their nearest and dearest in one of those homes longed to stage a fall down the stairs or something like it to put an end to this awful drain on the money they hoped to inherit.

'She was a druggie.'

Agatha started and swung round. Charles was

standing there. 'You mean the heiress?' said Agatha. 'How did you find out?'

'Entertained the maid, Gerda, on her evening off. You will get my bill. Yes, she had some dealer in Mircester. Know any?'

'I'll get Patrick onto it. Was Jennifer still seeing the bishop when she disappeared?'

'Nope. Told Gerda our bishop was a money-grabbing pillock.'

'There must be some good in him. He is collecting as much as he can for some old folks' home.'

Thunder rumbled in the distance. 'I wonder ...' Mrs Bloxby stared vaguely around her.

'Wonder what?' asked Charles.

'That dead policeman. Murdered. But everyone seems to have forgotten him and no one asks why he was killed.'

'I've been working on it,' lied Agatha, who did not want to admit to any flaw in her detective powers.

'And what has our great detective found out?' asked Charles.

'Someone didn't want his latest revelation to appear in the local paper.'

'And who was that someone, Sherlock?'

'I don't know,' said Agatha angrily. 'But it wouldn't amaze me if someone were murdered today. Wearing armour to ring bells! They're still ringing! I'm going back to have a look.'

The ringers were coming to the end of the peal. Mavis, a grotesque little figure in glittering armour was handling two sallies with ease. Must have muscles like iron, thought Agatha. All had removed their visors, and rivulets of sweat ran down their faces. All had looks of intense concentration. Millicent's expression could actually be described as exultation.

The thunder rumbled nearer and a gust of warm heavy wind blew in the open door of the bell tower. The last bell fell silent. The dean came in followed by a buxom woman carrying a large tray with tankards of beer.

'Excellent,' said the dean. 'Here is Gordon Fraser, who looks after the abbey museum, to help you again with the armour. I am sure you will be glad to get it off. And our cook, Mrs Rudge, with beer to cool you down.'

'I am surprised you allowed them to wear the armour,' said Agatha. 'Must be valuable.'

'Oh, these are replicas. We look after the originals very carefully. Mind you, these replicas are worth about two to five thousand pounds each. We hire them out for various occasions so they do pay their way. That is why the metal is very much lighter than the original would have been.'

'Who made them?' asked Agatha.

'A local man. Forget his name. Dead.'

'Of what?'

'What?'

'What did he die of?' asked Agatha.

'Botulism. Food poisoning.'

'Where from?'

'The abbey kitchens, if you must know.'

'Anyone else suffer?'

'No. Now I'm busy, Mrs Raisin.'

A gust of wind sent a shivery, sweet, single note down from the tenor bell.

Agatha went outside again and phoned Patrick who said he would chase up some drug dealers. In reply to another question he said no one had been found in connection with the dead policeman's murder and the pity of it was that Larry had been so unpopular that most people were just glad he was off the planet. Agatha said she could meet him in the bar of the George that evening.

Large plates of sandwiches had been supplied with the beer, which was very strong. Euphoria amongst the ringers changed to fatigue and then sulkiness and complaining.

'You should ha' rung my changes,' said Colin. 'But not you lot. Crawl to the bishop as usual.'

'It was stupid Helen fainting that caused the trouble,' said Gloria.

'Now, then,' said the dean. 'Birds in their little nests agree.'

'And what the fecking 'ell has that got to do with anything, you mad old bastard,' growled Harry Bury.

'A word, Mr Bury,' said Gordon, the armourer, leading him off into a corner and beginning to whisper. Harry turned a ruddy shade, nodded and went meekly back to join the others.

It's like the Mafia, thought Agatha suddenly, with the bishop as the consigliere and the other as his henchmen.

'Well, you all ought to thank me for saving the day,' said Mavis. 'Two bells! Did you see how I handled them?'

'Beautifully, dear lady,' said the bishop. 'Gordon, some more beer for our heroine.'

A huge buffet of wind blew into the chamber like an enormous sigh. The thunder rolled nearer. Agatha went back outside where the stall holders were busy packing up. 'Let's go back to the vicarage,' urged Mrs Bloxby. She had a feeling that if Agatha went to her cottage that wretched reporter might be waiting for her. Oh, it was so typical of the Agathas of this world who really did not think much of themselves to have their very first real love blasted on the vine. And there was Charles. He surely felt something for Agatha. Friendship was a safer basis for marriage. She was about to invite Charles to the vicarage as well but found it not necessary as he had obviously invited himself.

Settled comfortably in the vicarage drawing room, Agatha said, 'I never want to see that village again. I cannot understand why Helen Toms does not get a divorce.'

'She wouldn't have anything left to feel martyred about,' said Charles. 'And she would be free to marry Julian and that means sex and she doesn't like the idea.'

'How do you know?' demanded Agatha. 'Tried it on?'

'Experience,' said Charles.

'Unless you plan to stop detecting,' said Mrs Bloxby, 'I think you might be seeing Thirk Magna again.'

'What makes you say that?' Agatha's thoughts flew to Terry.

'Too many tense and emotional people. It is odd because bell ringers are usually very sane people.'

'Are you sure?' asked Charles. 'If I had to memorise all those mathematical changes, I'd go bonkers. Besides, may I point out that sane people do not dress up in armour on a sweaty day to pull sallies in a bell tower. Ah, I have news for you, Aggie.'

'Don't call me—'

'Shut up and listen. On the road here, Gerda the maid called me. She ferreted around Jennifer's old room and found a phone number written on the wallpaper behind the bed. So, I phoned it before I came in here.'

'And?'

'And, my peremptory and bulging-eyed sweetheart, I am going to meet her in the George bar at five o'clock. Turns out to be an old friend of Jennifer's.'

'I'll come, too.'

'No, you may sit in a corner and observe.'

'What's her name?'

'Ducksy Devenham. Nickname. Ducksy, that is. I think she's really called Sophy. I know the family. Very rich.'

Oh, Charles, thought Mrs Bloxby, don't start thinking of marriage, not until Agatha gets over that wretched reporter.

Later on that day, Agatha sat in a corner of the bar while Charles sat up at the bar talking to a leggy blonde. She looked out of the window as people scurried along the street in the driving rain. It was odd how the first six months of the year went galloping past. First it was the boat race, then the Derby, then suddenly the Trooping of the Colour and then people saying, 'Aren't the nights drawing in!'

Why don't I just chuck everything and go to Australia with Terry? she thought. People get divorced the whole time. But the children! Can't do that to the children. A large tear rolled down Agatha's cheek and dropped into her gin and tonic.

Ducksy was being helped into her coat by Charles. 'So that's a date,' Agatha heard her say. 'Din-dins here tomorrow night.'

Charles escorted her to the door and then returned and sat down next to Agatha.

'She is newly divorced,' said Charles, 'but is letting out only tiny bits of information about Jennifer because she wants to get married again. I am sure you are very grateful to me for all my detecting,' Charles went on, 'but have you forgotten that in Toni and Simon you have two young, clever and eager detectives?'

'No, of course not,' said Agatha, who had in fact forgotten practically everything in her misery. 'I'll get them to do some groundwork. Patrick will clue them in about the drug scene. If you found out where she went to get the drugs, even if she won't give you the name of Jennifer's supplier, Toni or Simon can go along and try to find out and maybe come across some more friends of Jennifer's.'

'Mind you,' said Charles, his eyes glinting sideways at Agatha, 'if I did marry dear Ducksy, it would be the end to my financial worries.'

'Why not?' Agatha shrugged. 'Thanks, Charles. I am so tired. I am going home.'

She walked off and Charles stared after her. He suddenly wished someone would murder someone or something would break to get Agatha's mind off that wretched reporter. The weather seemed set to stay rainy and dull. He knew that Agatha, not getting very far with the disappearance of Jennifer despite his efforts, would become bored with the daily round of missing cats, dogs and teenagers and all the other dreary grunt work of the agency.

That was the trouble with this thing called love. Whatever powerful chemicals it lets loose in the brain, it could make a saint justify a massacre. I hope it never happens to me, thought Charles. I am too fond of being in control. And yet ... maybe just a hint of what that glory would be like. Just a hint.

When Agatha returned to the cottage and let herself in, she found a note from Doris Simpson on the hall table. It said, 'These flowers arrived this afternoon. Letter included.'

Yellow roses, one dozen. She opened the accompanying letter.

'Darling,' she read, 'I am moving back with the family tomorrow evening to Australia. Please see me one more time. Can you meet me at El Vino's in Fleet Street tomorrow morning, to say good-bye? I love you. Terry.'

She experienced a feeling of almost sick exaltation. She would go. She was justified in going because it was one last time.

And yet to justify the time off that the visit would mean, she telephoned Toni and told her to concentrate on finding out where Jennifer might have gone to get drugs and who her friends might have been.

She did not feel like microwaving anything for dinner and so she fed her cats and then drove the short distance to the pub. She ordered lasagne and settled down at a corner table, opened a detective story and began to read.

'I know all about you,' hissed a voice. Agatha found herself looking into the face of Millicent Dupin, a face contorted with hate. 'It's women like you, sluts, who break up marriages. Poor Mrs Fletcher, and pregnant, too. Thank goodness she called on our dear friend the bishop and he was able to persuade the family to relocate to Australia.'

'Piss off!' shouted Agatha.

The pub fell silent. 'Get out of my face or I'll kill you, you nasty interfering bitch. God, I wish you would just drop dead.'

Mavis Dupin came hurrying up. 'Leave her alone. Us Dupins do not consort with harlots.'

'Listen, you dried-up freaky twosome, just go away and in future mind your own business or I will happily murder the pair of you.'

They stalked off.

I am still going, Agatha vowed. One more time. I deserve it.

But the next morning, with rain weeping and dripping from the thatch, she opened the door of her cottage to face Bill Wong and Alice Peterson.

'Mrs Agatha Raisin,' said Bill formally. 'You are to accompany us to headquarters for questioning regarding the murder of Millicent Dupin.'

'What? Why?' cried Agatha. I was going to my love, she mourned.

'Just come with us and everything will be explained.'

At police headquarters, it transpired that Millicent had told her sister that she was sure she saw someone going into the bell chamber. Mavis said she had already undressed and prepared for bed. Millicent took a torch and the key to the bell chamber and went out on her own. Mavis took her usual sleeping pill and did not awaken until six in the morning, her usual time of rising. The sisters slept together as they had always done and Mavis noticed that Millicent's nightdress was still folded on her pillow and her side of the bed did not show any signs of being slept in. She said she put on her dressing gown and went through the house calling for Millicent. The kitchen door was standing open and rain was blowing in. She ran to the bell tower and there she found her sister with her head smashed in, lying on the floor.

She had fainted but, when she pulled herself together, she went back to the house and called the police. When they arrived, she told them of Agatha's threats. Worse was to come for Agatha. Later on, Mavis spoke to the press. The days when reporters would have protected one of their own had long gone. Terry's infatuation for Agatha was printed for all to see. And what a tacky, cheap, little affair it looked in black-and-white.

Agatha wanted to leave the country but the police had her passport. She booked herself into a large tourist hotel in Falmouth and wondered if it were possible to die of shame.

Agatha had left her address with Doris in the hope that Charles might join her, but he never even phoned and, when she tried to contact him, Gustav blocked all her calls, saying Charles had gone abroad.

Two days after she had checked into the hotel, on a bleak Saturday with steady rain pockmarking the grey sea, she received a visit from Toni and Simon and Patrick Mulligan as well.

Agatha escorted them to the glassed-in terrace overlooking the sea and ordered coffees all round.

'Look!' exclaimed Toni. 'A patch of blue sky.'

And out on the horizon, sure enough, a patch of blue was growing bigger and bigger.

Agatha felt some of her shame and black misery roll away.

'First of all,' said Toni, 'you are no longer the number-one suspect. It seems that Millicent had a big crush on Bishop Peter and was apt to visit ladies of his parish and threaten them. Like you, they all said things like, "Piss off or I'll cut your head off and feed it to the pigs." That was said in the abbey by Mrs Weld-Pilkingon in front of the congregation. And that is just one example. They all make your threats look weak, Agatha. So, I got your passport back.'

'I felt such a fool,' muttered Agatha.

'Then forget about the coffee and have a gin and a cigarette. I bet you've been wearing a sort of hair shirt,' said Toni.

Agatha gave a weak smile. She had done a deal with the God she only half believed in that if he could spare her any more shame and blame, she would give up alcohol and smoking. So, she let Toni order a double gin and tonic for her and gratefully lit up a cigarette. Smoking was allowed on the terrace.

One of the elderly residents glared at Agatha, and muttering under her breath opened one of the windows. A frisky warm little breeze danced in, bringing with it the sound of the waves.

'How is Charles?' Agatha asked.

'He found out that Jennifer had fallen for some American preacher before she disappeared. That friend of Jennifer's, Ducksy, said she was crazy about him and that the bishop was a phony and that this man really believed in God.'

'And so Charles is following up that lead?'

There was an awkward silence and then Simon said, 'We thought you would know. It's in the papers this morning.'

'Never tell me he's gotten engaged to that Ducksy creature!'

'Well, he was worried about money. These estates eat money and then, with Brexit, he doesn't know if he'll still get any farm subsidies. We are all invited to the wedding.'

'This is all very quick. I dealt with his debts. *I helped him!*' Agatha's voice had risen at the end. She flushed and said in a lower tone of voice, 'He might have told me.'

Then she gave a mental shrug. It was time to revert to being Agatha Raisin again, successful businesswoman. But were women always cursed somewhere in their DNA with a longing for a man to look after them?

'I think I'll check out and go back to Mircester at the same time as you,' she said. 'What are they saying about Millicent's murder? I mean, I don't even know how she was murdered.'

'A simple bash on the head with a blunt instrument. They think it was a hammer,' said Patrick. 'Same sort of thing that killed Larry. The trouble with Larry was he couldn't keep it in his pants and it turns out there were a lot of men on and off the force who would have liked to see him dead.'

'I haven't been working hard enough,' said Agatha. 'My mind has just not been on work lately. Anyway, how's James? Don't tell me he's getting married as well.'

'Not him,' said Patrick, flashing a warning look at Simon. Patrick had heard from Phil who lived in Carsely that James had been dating a newcomer to the village but he felt that Agatha had borne enough for one morning.

'I came with Simon and Patrick,' said Toni, 'but why

don't I travel back with you, Agatha, and we can sit in your cottage and go over your notes. We might hit on something. Or visit Mrs Bloxby. People do talk to her.'

Agatha told herself that she felt *saner* than she had done for days and days. All the rapture she had felt over her affair with Terry seemed like a burst of madness.

She collected her cats from Doris's husband and let herself and Toni into her cottage, glad to be home and to believe herself cured.

Let Charles do what he wanted. She had wasted too many thoughts on that feckless man.

She smiled and stretched. Toni's voice came from the kitchen. 'I'll just let the cats out into the garden.'

'I'm having a G and T,' Agatha called from the sitting room. 'What about you?'

'Vodka and orange if you have it.'

'Coming right up.'

There was a silence and then Toni heard broken sounds and *no no no*s whispered over and over again.

She ran to the sitting room. Agatha was blocking the doorway, whimpering and shaking.

Toni pushed past her and stared in shock at the scene that met her eyes.

She recognised Terry Fletcher, despite the fact that his face was a mass of blood. He was still clutching a bouquet of yellow roses and one dead green eye stared mutely into space, the other having been drowned in a little river of blood from a savage wound on his head.

Chapter Six

Charles Fraith was not a happy man. His study at Barfield House was his favourite refuge, but now it had been invaded by his bride-to-be. Their respective lawyers were shortly due to arrive to discuss the marriage settlements.

'I'm bored. I'm going to turn on that telly,' said Ducksy. 'There's an Australian soap I want to see. Have you seen it? It's called *Live the Life*. There is this too-gorgeous surfer. My dear. Such pecs. Where's the remote?'

'I don't know,' said Charles, rustling his newspaper. 'Gustav hid it.'

'Oh, yes, that's another thing, my precious. We need to talk about what happens to Gustav.'

'Here's the remote,' said Charles, fishing it out from under a cushion next to him where he had hidden it.

'Ta. There's about ten minutes' news first. So dismal. I'll leave the sound off. Wait a minute. I saw that woman in the bar of the George the first night I met you. Hey!'

For Charles had seized the remote and turned up the sound. Agatha was being taken in for questioning over the murder of a reporter, Terry Fletcher. Charles gazed in horror at Agatha's white face and said, 'I've got to go.'

'The lawyers!'

'Get Gustav to cancel everything for the day.'

'Charles! I can sue you for breach of promise.'

But the slamming of the door was the only answer.

Chief Inspector Wilkes was a disappointed man as piece after piece of evidence arrived to show that Agatha Raisin could not have murdered Terry Fletcher. She had her booking at the hotel and petrol receipts and roadside restaurants for the journeys down and back from Cornwall.

But Agatha felt it was as bad as being found guilty. Her quickly summoned lawyer had told her that Mrs Fletcher had appeared on television, blaming Agatha for the breakup of her marriage. Agatha realised that she would probably have to move out of the Cotswolds altogether. Her badly damaged reputation would affect the business of the agency. And she would be damned forever as a breaker of marriages.

How had he got into Agatha's cottage? It turned out Doris's husband had let him in, but did not tell Agatha because Terry had made it sound like a romantic surprise and Mr Simpson had heard nothing about Agatha's scandalous affair.

She left the police station late that evening with Toni to find Charles waiting outside.

He didn't say anything, just put an arm around her

shoulders. 'I'll drive you home,' he said. 'Toni can fetch you in the morning. Didn't they offer you a police car?'

'Couldn't bear it,' said Agatha. 'Anyway, it'll need to be the George. I can't go home for a bit with forensics crawling all over the place and "make yourself ready for questioning, Mrs Raisin" being shot at me. Thanks, Toni. Just put my case in the boot. Thank goodness I've got luggage with me.'

Agatha booked one of the hotel suites on the top floor, feeling that, as she would be in the hotel for a while, she would need the space. Doris had taken her cats home with her, but Agatha found herself missing their furry company and, despite the hotel's no-pets policy, hoped to sneak them in.

'You can go now, Charles,' said Agatha. 'Strangely enough, I think I will be able to sleep.'

'In a while,' said Charles, beginning to pace up and down. 'Did Fletcher's wife have a good alibi?'

'Evidently. Never near the Cotswolds. Never left London. They were due to leave for Australia on the following day.'

'Agatha, if you had been there, I feel you would have been the one getting murdered. There seems to be a sort of hysterical hatred behind all this. And somehow, it all comes back to our bishop. He romances a lot of silly biddies to get money out of them for his old folks' home and they go bonkers and see you as a rival. Has to get rid of you and comes across Terry instead so he gets it.'

'Charles!' Agatha clutched his sleeve, and whispered, 'Someone is standing behind the door.'

She pointed with a shaking finger. The light was in the passage outside, brighter than the dimmer lamplight inside the suite. Charles could see, under the gap at the bottom of the door, the shadow of a pair of trousered legs.

He ran nimbly forward and jerked open the door. 'Good evening, sir,' said Gustav.

'What on earth are you doing here?'

'I assumed, sir, that you had gone to join Mrs Raisin because your fiancée told me about the news on television, and knowing that Mrs Raisin could not yet return home, I assumed she would be at the George.'

'Yes, well, push off.'

'I gather this suite has two bedrooms and I packed a case for you. Or I can drive you home.'

'Oh, sit down, Gustav,' said Agatha, guessing that Charles's engagement was causing trouble and wanting to hear about anything other than dead Terry. 'Before you do, get me a brandy out of the mini bar and open that window. I am going to smoke. And then help yourself.'

'Thank you, madam. But there is no need to open the window. The night has turned unseasonably chilly. I have become expert at disabling smoke alarms.'

'Let me see you do it.'

Gustav was tall. He reached up his long arms and simply jerked the smoke alarm so that it swung crazily on two wires.

'That's vandalism and I'll get billed for it,' complained Agatha.

'I always say that it just fell down,' said Gustav. 'No one has ever contradicted me.'

Agatha was beginning to feel she had wandered into the Mad Hatter's tea party. But she gratefully lit up a cigarette, thinking that British prices for tobacco were now so enormous that the fags ought to be gold plated. Charles and Gustav had brandies as well, helped themselves to Agatha's cigarettes and settled into armchairs.

'Oh, do make yourself at home,' said Agatha sarcastically. 'Don't let's even think about murder.'

'No, indeed,' said Gustav solemnly. 'There are more immediate and serious concerns.'

'Like what?'

'Miss Devenham plans to fire me. I told her you would not allow it. She asked why.'

There was a long silence while Gustav hunched forward, cradling his brandy glass between knobbly fingers and staring at the floor.

'Out with it, man. What did you say?'

'I said you would never get rid of me.'

'Yes, for what reason?'

'I said we were lovers, sir. Miss Devenham was sick on the carpet, sir. Then she ran away. She crashed her car at that ash tree at the bottom of the drive, but only a few cuts and bruises were the result. The doctors at Stratford hospital and the nurses were most sympathetic, especially a Dr Clearly who said he was gay as well and that Miss Devenham should be more understanding.'

'Gustav! Have you run mad? Of course I will sack you now. So, is the engagement off?'

'I am sure if you explain, sir, that I lied out of fear and distress, she will understand. She really does want to get married and she finds it hard to do so. It is said that in moments of ecstasy the young lady smells like stale kippers, very strong and pungent. Lady Sutcombe's carer told me as much. Said Tommy Gresham couldn't believe it and thought the cat had left some old fish under the bed. But he spoke later to Jimmy Talbot and he said, no, it was definitely her and it was all he could do to stop himself from shooting his cookies, which is an American expression, Mr Talbot hailing from Nantucket.'

'To think she was going on like the veriest virgin with me,' explained Charles. 'I don't care what she stinks of. I need that money. I know you helped me out, Agatha, but it doesn't seem fair.'

'Look, you precious pair,' said Agatha. 'I have just found a dead body in my sitting room and all you can do is talk about some deb who stinks of kippers but you don't mind because you need the money.'

Charles looked at Agatha's white, strained face. 'Off you go, Gustav,' he said quietly. 'Okay. Send a notice to the papers. Engagement off. Or does anyone bother announcing one these days?'

'I do not believe so. Thank you for the brandy, Mrs Raisin. I would like to say—'

'Just go,' said Charles.

When Gustav had left, Charles said, 'Come on, Aggie. Let's get you to bed.'

With his help, Agatha staggered to her feet and then fainted dead away. Charles lowered her back into an armchair and called for a doctor. The doctor gave her a heavy sedative. After the doctor had left, Charles got her into bed by efficiently stripping off her clothes and putting her nightgown on.

'Never fainted before,' mumbled Agatha. 'Thought you had to wear corsets to faint.' And that was the last thing she said for the rest of the night.

Charles phoned Toni the next morning to come and look after Agatha and then he went in search of Ducksy. He suspected that if he let Agatha go on handling his financial affairs and if he did not marry anyone else, then he might marry Agatha. And that, he firmly believed, would be the end of a friendship.

He was just standing outside the hotel when the bishop's palace limousine, driven by the dean, sailed past. In the backseat were Bishop Peter and Ducksy.

Setting off in pursuit, once he had remembered where he had parked his car, Charles did wonder what on earth he was going to say.

The palace had once been a great medieval house and only parts of its former grandeur could be seen. The great hall was divided up into sections with cheap board partitions where various charities had small offices: offices for the Mothers' Union, the Women's Institute, the Book Reading Group and so on. The building itself had been rebuilt in a neo-Tudor style, looking every bit as fake as Ye Olde English Tea Shoppe in the courtyard.

But linked to the palace was Bishop Peter's pride and joy, the chapel of St Mary, mostly used in preference to the abbey for ecclesiastical services. It had two beautiful fourteenth-century stained glass windows and a magnificent Baroque wooden pulpit carved by Grinling Gibbons.

Charles saw the bishop's Bentley was parked outside. He approached the entrance to the chapel and found his way blocked by the dean. 'Wrong way,' said Dean Whitby. 'This way.'

Charles had never been in this section of the abbey and found himself suddenly thrust into some sort of medieval cell. An oak door was slammed, a key was turned and the dean's voice came through a grille on the door. 'I'll let you out when there is no chance of you interfering. Just sit down in that nice cell. The prison was originally for felonious priests.'

'I'll sue you for unlawful imprisonment,' said Charles.

'Oh, yes? And I will say that the bishop and I were protecting Miss Devenham from a homosexual who only wants to marry her for her money.'

'I am not a homosexual!' raged Charles.

'So hard to prove these days, is it not?'

And with that, the dean walked off, laughing.

Charles took stock of his situation. He wondered if the dean had left the key in the door. In the boys' books of his youth, boys were always escaping by putting a handkerchief under the door, pushing the key onto it and drawing it through.

After examination, he discovered the key was indeed in the door but no amount of poking and pushing would make it fall.

Then, as a last resort, he tried the handle, and found that the Dean had forgotten to lock it.

Charles was just leaving the cell when he saw bundles of old newspapers stacked against the wall outside. He bent down and felt them. They were tinder dry. He set fire to the lot and fled before the flames could block his way. Smoke billowed after him down the corridor. The dean erupted through the smoke, howling, 'What have you done?'

Charles punched him as hard on the nose as he could, skirted round him and managed to find a way out into the courtyard.

Ducksy was in the middle of the courtyard in the arms of the bishop. Peter gazed into her eyes and said, 'Do you feel the ecstasy of the spirit?'

'Oh, yes, *darling*,' said Ducksy, and Peter screwed up his face before a sudden waft of rotting kippers.

Charles gave up in that moment. He felt ridiculous at even having contemplated marriage. He would go back home and get Gustav to shut out all visitors.

But he should not have been as surprised as he was a week later when, venturing out for the first time to join Agatha, who had been allowed back into her cottage, he got the news on his phone from Gustav that an engagement had been announced between Bishop Peter Salver-Hinkley and Miss Sophy Devenham.

'She must be really awfully rich,' said Agatha.

'Gustav just found out. Daddy is First Plastico.'

'What's that?'

'It is a form of biodegradable plastic. All that rubbish polluting the sea just melts away. The family is worth millions, Aggie.'

'Don't call m—'

'Oh, God, and I threw it all away to go rushing to your side. Brings tears to my eyes. So, let's talk murder.'

'I want to come over!' called a voice over the garden fence.

'Over you come, James,' shouted Agatha.

James Lacey nimbly scaled the high fence that blocked Agatha's garden from his own to join them round Agatha's garden table. 'You should lower that fence, Agatha,' he said. 'It blocks out the sunlight from half our gardens. Charles, I see your ex-fiancée is to wed the bishop,' said James. 'There's talk that Peter Salver-Hinkley wants the whole of his palace restored to its original glory.'

'He should have waited until they were actually married. I never saw the marriage settlements but I gather they were pretty stiff. I don't think he'll be able to touch her money,' said Charles.

'If you knew all that, why on earth were you so keen to marry her to settle your debts?' demanded Agatha.

116

'I dunno. Thought I could be the one to winkle some of it out of the family coffers. Father is a bully. Takes all the credit for plastic and gives long boring speeches about how he discovered it although it was actually discovered by Wayne something, a dweeb in the lab.'

Agatha looked at him. He was as impeccably barbered and tailored as usual. There was something almost oriental about his imperturbability. She wondered what he really felt.

As if conscious of her gaze, Charles turned and stared at her for a long minute as if trying to make up his mind about something. Then he said, 'Time for drinks. After eleven in the morning on a Saturday. No, don't get up, Agatha. Give me a hand, James, and we'll just wheel the drinks trolley into the garden.'

Agatha looked at her packet of cigarettes on the garden table. All over the place, people were giving up smoking. Why couldn't she? Well, she would resist this morning and take it from there.

But Charles helped himself to a whisky and soda, opened Agatha's packet of cigarettes, extracted one, lit it up and blew a lazy smoke ring up to drift among the roses. That was it. Agatha followed suit. The doorbell rang. James went to answer it and came back with Bill Wong and Alice Peterson. Agatha repressed a sigh. She could remember, although she was much older than Bill, when she was the only female in his life, although not romantically, thanks to his parents scaring anyone else who came near. But Bill was so much in love with Alice that he had at last moved out of the family home and had stood up to his parents for the first time.

'Now what?' asked Agatha.

'We wondered if you knew about this,' said Bill.

'About what?'

'Mrs Fletcher.'

'Oh, for pity's sakes, what's the wretched woman whining about now? Does she expect me to go around wearing sackcloth and ashes?'

'Evidently not. She had a very strong alibi for the day her husband was murdered.'

'Like what?'

'Like she had a friend pick the kids up from play-school while she rollicked in bed with Terry's best friend, Jerry Milne. They then went to Melbourne together and they are to be married tomorrow.'

'The guilt that woman caused me! Hey! You didn't believe that alibi. You can't rollick around when you are so far gone in pregnancy.'

'Sometimes Agatha's innocence can be quite touching,' said Charles.

'Well, canoodle or rollick,' said Alice. 'She did.'

'I mean, you are taking her word for it?'

'No, her neighbour, Mrs Josie Burns. She said they did not pull the curtains and pranced about in the nude together.'

'Surely that's fishy,' said James. 'I mean, they are making pretty sure they have an alibi, maybe even before he landed dead on Agatha's carpet. When did he die exactly?'

118

'From the stomach contents, about two hours after a hamburger which he bought in the Red Lion had been digested. And during those two hours was when Mrs Burns saw what she called "disgusting behaviour. Like the fall of Rome."'

'There's a programme on the telly called *The Fall of Rome*,' said the voice of Roy Silver, Agatha's former employee, from the doorway. 'It's a toga ripper.'

'Come in, Roy. Who left the door open?'

'I must have done,' said Bill.

'It can't be very sexy ripping togas,' said Agatha. 'Fellows wear togas.'

'It's to celebrate gay people in the arts,' said Roy. 'Where are all the press?'

'Don't you of all people read the newspapers? Better stories elsewhere.'

'But this place has never been out of the headlines,' complained Roy. 'They've named it Death Village. I heard all the press were here from Japan to *Paris Match*.'

'It's like this,' explained James. 'Horrible news all round. Massive shooting in a school in Texas, the worst ever. Supermarket hostages all night in Marseilles and a mosque in Belgium set on fire with the worshippers locked inside. So, every journalist packed up. They've been writing the same thing here over and over again.'

Agatha could feel a warm sensation of relief coursing through her body. Mrs Fletcher would be all right now. She tried to remember the power and the glory of her feelings for Terry and could not experience them again.

She felt she had a new perspective on Terry's murder.

She was now sure that not only Terry but his wife were possibly amoral. Terry may have seduced a colleague's wife. 'Bill,' she ventured, 'isn't it possible that Mrs Fletcher paid for Terry to be killed?'

'We thought of that. But she didn't seem to have those sorts of connections.'

'Oh, well, I wonder if I will be invited to the bishop's wedding,' said Agatha.

'I saw his photo,' said Roy. 'You simply must introduce me, Agatha. He is gorgeous.'

Agatha sighed. 'Now that the stigma of marriage breaker has been taken away from me, or will be tomorrow when the newspapers report Mrs Fletcher's wedding, it means I don't need to sell my cottage. I think I know where we can find the bishop this evening, Roy.'

'Be careful,' warned Charles. 'That dean of his is a thug. I think I might have broken a little bone on my finger when I socked him on the nose. I'll come with you.'

'I should think the Greek restaurant is a good place to start,' said Agatha.

When Roy came downstairs that evening, Agatha surveyed his evening outfit of pale blue jacket with three-quarter sleeves, pink shirt and jeans with holes torn in the knees. 'You look so retro, Roy. If you wore an ordinary suit and took that gel out of your hair, you would look very much younger.'

'I knew it would happen eventually!' cried Roy.

'You've finally gone countryfied. You'll be wearing tweed knickers next. Let's just go. I'm hungry. What's the food like?'

'Awful!'

'So why are we going there?'

'Because,' said Agatha, 'you've fallen for the bishop and I am detecting.'

It had been a fine summer's day, but the evening had turned cold and drizzly. 'Zorba the Greek' was thudding out from the Greek restaurant. 'Can I smash plates?' asked Roy.

They entered the restaurant. Only a couple of men were customers. The rest of the tables were empty. Agatha saw the Glaswegian waiter approaching.

'Devils for punishment,' he said cheerfully. 'Whit's it tae be?'

'What about some menus, matey,' said Roy in what he thought was a sort of bloke-to-bloke voice.

'Weel, matey, the menu is up there on the blackboard. I waud hae the stuffed vine leaves although they're cabbage leaves but the stuff's fresh.'

Agatha suggested that they all have some garlic bread and wine and then go somewhere afterwards where they could get a decent meal. 'Is the bishop coming tonight?' she asked.

'Oh, aye, all the biddies'll be here and he'll be trying to get money offa them. It's a fund-raiser for the auld folks.'

'What time?'

'Nine o' clock.'

'Bit late for the elderly,' said Charles.

'I heard that dean say that the plum picking couldnae get here any earlier.'

'It's an odd thing,' said Agatha, 'the way he is so determined to provide a home for the elderly. I mean, quite honestly, I can't imagine him having a charitable bone in his body. Also, we never really looked up why he was adopted and where he was adopted from.'

'I know that one,' said Charles. 'Met Lady Fathering last year. Her best friend, Molly Hepworth, got pregnant after some wild party. Her parents were anti-abortion and so she had the child and there was Lady Fathering gasping for one and the deed was done. Husband, Henry, fought against it, but he was not firing on all cylinders so it wasn't as if he could give her one, so he learned to shut up although he does loathe our Peter.'

'My mind keeps going back to that dead policeman,' said Agatha. 'Surely the one person interested in getting rid of him is our bishop because Larry was, I am sure, about to sell stories about naughty vicars and sado-masochism to the newspapers.'

'That dean bothers me,' said Charles. 'He's a thug. Uh-oh, here he comes.'

A little procession, headed by the bishop, entered the restaurant. Bishop Peter led the way with Ducksy on his arm. Behind her with the dean came Mavis Dupin, darting angry little looks into Ducksy's back. Behind her walked three women and one man.

122

Peter said something to Ducksy and came over to their table. He kissed Agatha's hand and gazed into her eyes. 'Introduce me,' hissed Roy.

Agatha made the introductions. 'That purple does suit you,' gushed Roy. 'Ever so flattering.'

'And so are you,' said Peter. 'Are you a detective as well?'

'He's in public relations,' said Agatha.

'I can speak for myself, sweetie,' said Roy.

'There's a coincidence,' cried Peter. 'I am raising money for an old folks' home but we have never achieved the necessary publicity.'

'I've got some ideas,' said Roy eagerly.

'Wonderful! If Agatha will excuse us . . .'

'Is Roy actually any good?' asked Charles. 'He always seems to be picking your brains.'

'Oh, yes, he loves that whole trashy world and revels in it. I am the one who is glad to get out of public relations.'

'Be careful. The bishop has just swivelled round to cast an enquiring eye in your direction.'

'He can cast as much as he likes. Mind you, it might be a way of getting something on missing Jennifer. Oh, here comes the first murderer – I mean, the dean. He's coming here.'

'Bugger off,' said Charles.

'I owe you one, said the dean placidly. 'Who's the spotty chappy with Peter?'

'I'll scratch your back, you scratch mine. Where's Jennifer Toynby?'

'I really, honest to God, don't know. One minute she was all over the place. Oh, this other preacher was a sort of Billy Graham. He was seated next to her at a dinner at the palace. Next day, she had gone.'

'I gather,' said Agatha, 'that the countrywide police hunt was immediate. Why?'

'Because all her clothes and wallet, purse, passport and house keys had been left behind, that's why. Last message texted to her mum said, "Getting out of this world."'

'I'd better go with my little brush and shovel to pick up the pieces.'

'From which one?'

'Ducksy. No amount of money could make anyone tolerate that dreadful smell.'

'He looks a bit standoffish,' said Charles. 'She only blooms in moments of rapture.'

'Okay. Pay some more attention to me and leave the Rainbow Alliance alone,' Ducksy was saying.

Under the checked tablecloth, he ran a hand up her leg, caressing and stroking. She wriggled and closed her eyes. Peter signalled the waiter. 'There is rotten fish under this table. Get rid of it. No, move us all to another table.'

'Could I hae a wee word in your ear, Your Eminence?' said the waiter.

'Can't it wait? Oh, very well.'

'The waiter is about to explain the smell,' said Charles.

'Surely not,' said Agatha.

''Fraid so. Gustav said dear Ducksy was apt to put it about a bit. Didn't believe him. But the dear bishop is now looking a whiter shade of pale. Think of all that money, man! Yes, he's thought. He is smiling on his beloved. Wait a bit! She is not smiling back.'

'A note was delivered to her,' said Agatha. 'She has read it and looked as surly as hell. Yes, she's getting up to leave.'

They watched Peter pleading with her, then getting angry and saying something, and that was when Ducky slapped him savagely across the whiteness of his face, leaving an angry red mark.

The dean took her arm in a strong grip and marched her from the restaurant. 'Good grief, I do believe he's going to lock her up in that cell he put me in!' exclaimed Charles.

Then, from outside the restaurant, came the sound of a shot, a man crying out and the sound of running feet. Agatha was the first outside the restaurant.

Dean Donald Whitby was lying on the ground, clutching his stomach, blood oozing through his fingers. While Agatha phoned for police and ambulance, Peter knelt down and cradled the dean's head. 'I'll make the bitch pay for this,' he said. 'Hang in there.'

Outside the restaurant was cordoned off after the dean had been taken off to hospital. It was then that they discovered the bishop was missing. 'He didn't go in the ambulance,' said Agatha.

'He went to search the palace,' said Roy eagerly as he watched the press arriving on the other side of the tape.

Police and detectives searched all night but there was no sign of Ducksy. The search widened to ports and airports but nothing could be found. Like Jennifer, she had disappeared, not even taking a passport with her.

'You would think the bloodhounds would have found her if that smell is as bad as reported.'

'And there's a lot of it,' said Charles. 'It's not an orgasm. She just needs to feel flattered and this awful body odour sours the air. Smells like rotting kippers.'

'Or red herrings,' said Roy and shrieked with laughter at his own wit. Then, when he judged the police were not looking, he nipped under the tape and could be seen busily talking to the press.

'Where is Peter?' asked Charles.

'The police have taken him away,' said Agatha. 'We'd better move. We're next to be grilled at headquarters but Alice is going to take our statements first and then we go tomorrow and sign the things. Here she comes. Alice, let's go back inside the restaurant where we can sit down and have a drink.'

Alice agreed. 'Wiz yiz be wantin yir vine leaves?' asked the waiter.

'May as well,' said Agatha. 'And a bottle of wine. Merlot.'

She turned to Charles. 'Did you know she carried a gun?'

'Of course not. I mean, this is Britain.'

126

'The things men will do and the lengths they will go for money is sickening,' said Agatha.

Roy came hurrying to join them, tears running down his face. Pimples stood out red again the pallor of his skin. Agatha had a sudden mad impulse to take out a pen and play 'join the dots'. Instead she asked, 'What happened?'

'I was talking to the reporters and this policeman came up and snarled at me to join you and I said, "In a minute, my good man." Polite, see? He stamped on my foot and I think he's broken a bone. He said, "Shut up and do as you're told, poofter."'

Alice said, 'Excuse me,' and slid from the table, only to return in a few moments with a brute of a policeman who had to humbly apologise to Roy.

Roy, delighted to be the centre of attention and finding his foot didn't hurt anymore, graciously forgave the policeman and only Alice, interrupting to say she really wanted to get their statements, had the effect of shutting him up.

The 'vine leaves' were cabbage stuffed with glutinous rice. Agatha paid the waiter and tipped him so that he could go to the nearest Marks & Spencer and buy them a selection of sandwiches. Alice was a calm and efficient interviewer with a soothing manner but Agatha's mind turned and churned with unanswered questions. Why had Ducksy been carrying a gun?

The waiter came back with a bag of sandwiches. To Agatha's fury, he not only picked out one of the better sandwiches for himself but sat down at the table and joined them.

Charles looked amused. 'As the Victorians used to say, know your place, my good man.'

'Or as I would say, haggis face,' hissed Agatha, 'get lost.'

'Oh, weel, and here's me just figured out what caused that awfy smell o' hers.'

'I'll see you all at headquarters in the morning,' said Alice. 'I'll type up your statements ready for you to sign.'

Agatha stared at the waiter. 'Okay. But I thought it was because she was sexually aroused.'

'Naw, it was when she was scared.'

'You mean like a skunk!' said Roy.

'Could be. But take ma word for it. It's the vodka. Awfy stuff. In some folk that drinks it day and nicht, it comes up through the skin wi' the worst stink this side o' hell. If fear makes them sweat, then you get the aroma o' dead kippers.' He reached for another sandwich but Agatha slapped his wrist.

'So obviously it was any intimacy that frightened her,' said Charles. 'So why get married?'

'It's them lesbians. Some o' them waud rather stay in the closet.'

'In this day and age!' said Roy. 'How bizarre.'

'If all she wanted was the outward appearance of marriage, why didn't she say so?' said Charles. 'I'd have married her like a shot.'

'Dream on,' snapped Agatha. 'I bet the marriage

128

settlement would have bankrupted you. Oh, let's get back to all this business. Heiress goes missing, now Ducksy, another one goes missing. What have they in common? Both engaged to Peter. Our bishop has a thuggish dean. Maybe he is the reason Ducksy carried a gun.'

Charles stifled a yawn. 'We can't do anything tonight. That wine is Chateau Yesterday. Make it in the bathtub, waiter? No. Don't answer that. On second thoughts I just don't want to know.'

To Agatha's relief, Roy decided to drive back to London and Charles, too, said he would go home.

She had showered before bed but lifted an arm and sniffed it cautiously. Did gin make one smell? How would poor Ducksy ever know? Men wouldn't tell her. They would just drop her. Was she really a lesbian? That was the sort of thing men usually said when they got a rejection.

She sat on the kitchen floor with her cats on her lap, wondering why she could not be content with her own company, always looking for some man to fill the hole in the soul.

Her mobile phone rang. She looked at the dial. It was Julian Brody. Agatha answered it, reluctantly as she felt tired and just wanted to go to bed.

'I'm outside,' said Julian. 'I'll only take a few minutes of your time.'

Agatha lifted each cat onto the floor and went to open the front door. It dawned on her again that Julian was a very good-looking young man.

'Come in,' she said. 'It has been quite an evening.'

'I heard all sorts of things. What happened?'

Agatha gave him a concise summary up of the evening's events right down to the fact of Ducksy's odd body odour.

'That can't be right,' protested Julian. He had followed her through to the kitchen and was seated at the table with Hodge and Boswell on his lap. 'I mean, we all drink vodka because it *doesn't* smell.'

'I've just remembered I knew someone that vodka had the same effect on. You have to drink buckets of the stuff, mind you.' She stifled a yawn. 'Sorry, I am weary.'

'I do not understand women at all,' complained Julian. 'Helen won't divorce that husband of hers.'

'Stand by for this old chestnut. Maybe she's afraid of commitment. Maybe she doesn't like sex. I used to have lousy digs down the East End of London when I was a young woman. The girls were saucy and flirty up until they were married and then with the first pram they ran to seed and their friends would ask, "Does he bother you much?" And if she said, "No," they'd sigh with envy and say, "Aren't you lucky?" Because "yes" meant another squalling kid.'

'What about the birth control pill?'

'If the husband wants kids, the wife will get a beating for taking them. He won't use a condom because he says it's like having sex with your socks on.'

'Do you think you will ever get anything on Peter? I think it is his influence that is keeping Helen away from me.'

'I am sorry to say this,' said Agatha, 'but I think she's

a born martyr and she is never going to leave her husband but she likes keeping you on a string. Look! Try ignoring her. I bet she tries to get you back on the hook. And, so, do you want me to stop investigating?'

'Just a few more weeks. And you could do something else. Go out with me a couple of evenings to events that Helen will be at and look as if you are attracted to me. If she is jealous, then there is hope there.'

Agatha opened her mouth to refuse, but then the thought slid into her head. What if Charles could be made jealous? It would be interesting to find out. But he would need to be there as well.

'The annual charity ball is at Barfield House,' said Julian.

'Charles's home?'

'Fraith. Yes, holds one every year to raise money for disabled people. Lets the committee use the house but doesn't attend himself.'

'He just might if he knew I was there,' said Agatha. 'When is it?'

'Tomorrow evening.'

'I haven't got a ball gown.'

'It's not like *Strictly Come Dancing* on television, all sequins and net. A long skirt and blouse are all that is needed.'

Later, when Agatha lay in bed, common sense deserted her and teenage dreams of being Cinderella filled her mind. She knew Barfield House well and knew that one went downstairs to the ballroom. She would descend on

131

Julian's arm in a froth of rose chiffon with just a few sequins like stars twinkling in the light. She and Charles would announce their engagement, so went her dream, and Julian, who had actually fallen in love with her, would try not to cry. It would be like that wonderful evening when she was sixteen and she bought a standing-room ticket for a Covent Garden Opera touring company. The opera was *Eugene Onegin.* And, oh, how she gazed with her mouth open when Tchaikovsky's music swelled into the famous polonaise and the richly gowned dancers swirled onto the stage, filling it with beauty and colour. But then she remembered the awful comedown after all that beauty to have to go back to the slum where she lived with her parents, to noise and filth and the garbage-strewn stairwell and, of course, the lift that didn't work. Feeling the blackness inside her and the resentment that such visits to the opera were not for such as herself, and from then on growing older and harder and finding she could get what she wanted if she tried long enough, she somehow lost her innocence along the way and with it her appreciation of beauty. But she kept her talent for escaping into Walter Mitty dreams. Agatha fell asleep smiling, because that child was still somewhere inside, sheltered by ridiculous dreams and fantasies.

The next day, she emailed Charles to say she would be at the ball. He did not reply and Gustav had already refused to pass on any message.

Agatha looked up old photographs in *Cotswold Life* of

the ball. The gowns weren't very grand. So much for dreams. A velvet skirt and a rose chiffon blouse would do. 'Oh, why did I agree to this stupid idea?' she complained to Hodge and Boswell, who gave fur shrugs of cat indifference and slid off into the garden.

It was only when she was dressing for the ball that she realised she had not worked hard enough for Julian. Agatha began to speculate. She was sure that somehow the disappearance of Jennifer Toynby was connected to the murders of Millicent and Larry. And she was pretty sure the murderer was the bishop, or his dean acting on the bishop's commands. Say Jennifer had found out something, then it stood to reason that she had to go, if what she knew was dangerous for the bishop. Larry had found out about the sex games and, yes, that certainly would have damaged the bishop if it had got into the newspapers because it was Bishop Peter who had started the games.

Then she had never even interviewed this farmer, Lawrence Crowther, said to be Jennifer's fiancé. Now she knew why people talked of being shot by Cupid's arrow. It was a love close to madness.

The doorbell rang. Agatha gave her nose a final dusting of powder and went to answer it. Julian looked very handsome in formal dress and Agatha hoped that Charles would turn up at the ball. If he did, she also hoped it would be before Helen Toms put in an appearance because, once she arrived, it would be plain to everyone that Julian did not have eyes for anyone else.

Julian flattered Agatha on her appearance, and Agatha, who usually took compliments with little grace, forced herself to charm him, remembering he was a client and the fact that he fancied a drip like Helen Toms did not make him sub-normal.

The rain had stopped and the evening was full of the smell of roses and greenery. As they approached Barfield House and heard the thud of the music, Agatha began to dream that this was the evening when *he* would be waiting for her, that mysterious one she thought she had found in Terry. Poor Terry. Who on earth had killed him and why? That thought had been churning through her head for days now. What she had forgotten and now remembered was that he had enjoyed the reputation of a first-class reporter, having an acute intuition. She vowed that the next morning, she would go round Thirk Magna and question as many people as possible to see if Terry had talked to any of them and let fall some clue. And what about his photographer? Damn! She was slipping.

All this intense thinking had made her forget her surroundings and it was only the sound of the majordomo announcing her name that made her aware of the fact that she was about to descend into the ballroom. She could not see Charles anywhere.

Julian had seen Helen. 'I wonder, Agatha . . .' he began.

'Oh, go on. Make a fool of yourself,' said Agatha. 'I'm going to look for Charles.'

A noisy disco dance had just finished and Agatha was cutting across the dance floor when she was waylaid by a stocky young woman wearing a crumpled white dress and baseball boots.

'I'm Felicity Durne,' she boomed, thrusting her face forwards. She had bleached her moustache. Should have shaved, thought Agatha. 'And you are that detective, Agatha Raisin?'

'Yes? So?'

'I was going to ask you to join our group, Feminism Lives. Then I saw your shoes and dearie, dearie me. Stilettos! At your age? You're a disgrace to the cause. What have you got to say for yourself?'

Suddenly Agatha was engulfed with a wave of rage against the whole stupid world in general and this woman in particular.

'Oh, sod off, you creepy frump,' said Agatha.

Felicity punched Agatha on the nose. Agatha screamed with pain and kicked Felicity in the shins, seized a glass of red wine from the tray of a passing waiter and poured it down the woman's cleavage.

Charles was ensconced in his study, a book in his hand and his slippered feet on a footstool when his elderly aunt dithered into the room. 'You must rouse yourself, dear. Rouse, immediately. The Raisin woman is brawling in the ballroom.'

'Can't Gustav or the catering firm people stop it?'

'No, dear. The Raisin creature and Felicity Durne are locked in combat and everyone is cheering them on.'

'Drat the woman. It's all right, aunt. I'll stop it.'

* * *

135

In the ballroom, Charles thrust his way through the onlookers, grabbed Agatha, slung her over his shoulder and hurried from the ballroom while Felicity lay on the floor and screamed with rage.

He dumped Agatha on the floor of his study and said, 'Pull yourself together. Felicity is a pill. She's mad. No one but you would have paid any attention to her. I assume she insulted you. She's always insulting someone. Now, if you want a drink, get it yourself and then you may tell Uncle Charles why you came to this gig. Not your thing.'

Agatha helped herself to a gin and tonic, sat down in an armchair by the fire and told him fictitious reasons for attending. She could hardly tell him she wanted to see if he could be made jealous. 'There are people here I want to study. I gather from Julian that the bishop is here. Why on earth do you let that Felicity creature insult your guests?'

'Because no one but you has ever taken her seriously. Oh, well, let's go and dance. And, no, Agatha, I am not jealous. You should have chosen some other escort and not a man mooning over a drip of a vicar's wife. Why is this bishop so mad keen on the old folks' home?'

'I should think because there is a lot of money in them these days. It can cost one and a half thousand a week, you know, and then if he can charm some old bird, she might leave the family money to him. Have you ever met his adopted mother?'

'Lady Fathering, eldest daughter of the Earl of Hadshire? Once, in the south of France.'

'What was she like?'

'Loud, hard, seen too many old Noel Coward plays and has the long cigarette holder to prove it.'

'And the husband?'

'Harold Bisset, owned a chain of butcher shops. Sold out before the supermarkets started to woo away customers. Snob. Hints at a military background but ain't got one. She'd already adopted Peter.'

'Where did he come from?'

'Told you. Best friend's kid.'

'I should have been working on this,' complained Agatha. 'I'm slipping. Do you know, I haven't even questioned Terry's photographer.'

'Well, of course you wouldn't,' said Charles. 'Frightened to find out that the love of your life was just another fling to him?' Two large tears spilled out of Agatha's eyes and rolled down her cheeks.

'NO!' shouted Charles. 'Let's dance. I refuse to let you mourn.'

But as he whirled Agatha onto the dance floor, Charles thought that he, too, was forgetting the basic facts: that Larry had been murdered and then Millicent followed by Terry, and Terry had been murdered in Agatha's home. 'Enter, bishop and dean,' said Charles, looking over Agatha's shoulder. 'First and second murderer. They look furtive. What have they been up to?'

'Probably burying Ducksy where they have already buried Jennifer,' said Agatha. 'That awful smell! The police dogs should find her soon. I gather Ducksy's parents alerted the police after three days.'

'All this speculation about her "body odour", as my aunt calls it. She said that in her youth, there were advertisements for deodorant with a photo of one whispering to another, "You've got B.O.," followed by the legend, "Even your best friend won't tell you." I always wondered who the one telling the other in the photo was supposed to be. Now Gustav would say anything to put me off marriage.

'The dean thinks her smell is sexual, the waiter thinks her smell is vodka. I think it is very simple. I just worked it out.'

'That being?' asked Agatha. 'You mean she's a walking, talking red herring?'

'No. It is all so simple. She loves smoked fish. I have seen her eat two kippers for breakfast. And finnan haddie for dinner, cooked in milk with three poached eggs on top.'

'Are you sure? The world is full of idiots thinking that vodka doesn't smell. Of course, they think it doesn't smell of alcohol. Wrong! And if they sink a lot of the stuff, the most awful stink comes off them as if something had died inside.'

'Well, they haven't been able to find her. I'm sure that wretched dean has offed them?'

'Offed? You do have a way with words. Oh, they're playing "Hello Dolly" and I must dance.'

They moved onto the floor in a quickstep and Agatha began to sing, belting out the words.

'Making a spectacle of yourself,' said Charles. 'I am quite pink with embarrassment.'

'I am sorry,' said Agatha, suddenly aware of all the amused looks from the other dancers. 'I saw Barbra Streisand sing that when I was very young. I so wanted to be Streisand. No, I wanted to be Dolly. Oh, where's that coming from?'

'Where's what?'

'Menace,' said Agatha, half to herself. She looked around. Bishop Peter was dancing with Helen Toms and she was gazing up into his face like a woman bewitched while Julian leaned against a pillar and watched them with jealous eyes.

'It's like one of those Victorian paintings, you know: every picture tells a story. Does our bish make you tremble, Aggie?'

'Yes, with fear. I swear to God he's a murderer and I am going to prove it. Uh-oh, here he comes.'

'Mrs Raisin – Agatha – I beg the next dance,' said Peter.

'Oh, all right,' said Agatha with a marked lack of enthusiasm. But the bishop was a beautiful dancer and he looked handsome in formal dress and she soon began to enjoy herself.

'Been murdering anyone lately?' asked Agatha.

'Like Bluebeard,' he said. 'I am just getting around to my fortieth virgin.'

'Any sign of Ducksy?'

'Not even a whiff. But they found her passport so she is still in the country.'

'I am sure she will turn up in some crypt somewhere.'

'Agatha! You are so ghoulish!' He jerked her more

closely in his arms and she felt that wave of sexuality that he seemed able to turn on and off like a tap.

She jerked backwards just in time as a large china vase went sailing past, dangerously close to her head. There was a startled silence as the band fell silent.

Charles's aunt wailed, 'Uncle Arthur brought that back from Hong Kong.'

'Never mind,' said Charles. 'It's not Ming. You all right, Agatha?'

'That was meant for me,' she said. 'Who's up there?' Before Charles could stop her, she ran for the stairs to the gallery which overlooked the ballroom.

Charles ran after her, but not before he noticed the bishop was looking amused.

The gallery was empty.

Chapter Seven

Agatha left soon afterwards. She told Charles not to call the police. She'd had enough of questioning recently, she felt, to last her a lifetime. Also, everyone appeared to think that it had been Felicity Durne who had tried to throw the jar at her.

She trailed through to her kitchen. She had told Julian that she meant to go straight to bed. 'Where are you?' she called to her cats. 'Come on, furry rat bags. People food if you come now. Cat food if you don't.'

Agatha had never thought of herself as an animal lover. Bill Wong had given her Hodge and she had picked up Boswell in London, mistaking the tabby for Hodge who had gone missing. James had chosen the names. Agatha was told that Dr Johnson's cat was named Hodge and his friend and biographer had been Boswell. Agatha loathed the doctor's very name. He always seemed to be quoted in the Cotswolds by whippet-thin women who balanced with one hand on one hip, head thrown back, 'As the dear doctor would say . . .'

Opening the kitchen door, Agatha called into the darkness. 'Where are you?'

She experienced a sharp stab of fear. She ran down the garden, calling wildly. She ran back through her cottage, out the front door and banged on James's door, shouting 'Help!' at the top of her voice. A light went on in James's cottage and he leaned out of the stair window.

'James,' pleaded Agatha. 'Someone's taken my cats.'

'You're sure?'

'They've never, ever gone away before.'

'Go and phone the police. I'll be with you in a moment.'

She was turning away when she heard a female voice call, 'What's going on, darling?'

'Neighbour trouble. Go back to bed.'

The idea that her ex might be involved with someone did not trouble her at this moment. She phoned police headquarters and then roused her whole detective staff. James arrived to find Agatha slumped on the kitchen floor, tears running down her cheeks.

He handed her a large handkerchief and then went out into the garden, calling for the cats. Normally the police would ignore a call about missing cats, but Bill Wong, first of them to arrive, knew that if they had been taken, it was a threat against Agatha.

When her staff arrived, they soon left again to search the village.

A tall woman draped in a man's dressing gown came into the kitchen. She had blonde hair, high cheekbones and grey eyes. Even in her distress, Agatha recognised James's dressing gown. 'Where is James?' she asked.

Mrs Bloxby had just arrived. She went up to the

woman and whispered something urgently and then sat down on the floor next to Agatha and put an arm round her shoulders. 'Detective Wong is coming. I found him up the village. A note was put through my door.'

'What did it say?'

'Here he is.'

'Agatha,' said Bill. 'This is a ransom demand. Either you pay fifty thousand pounds by eleven o'clock tomorrow or your cats will be sent to you in pieces. Instructions on where to drop the money to arrive later.'

Agatha had once joked that all men from Glasgow seemed to be called Jimmy. But the waiter at the Greek restaurant was called Jimmy and he was in a rage. He had not received his wages. The manager had shrugged and said he hadn't any money to spare. The restaurant was closing down and was reopening as a curry house.

Jimmy hated the bishop with a passion but he was afraid of the dean. He decided that theft in this case was legitimate. He collected his skeleton keys, let himself into the palace and headed for the bishop's office. He cursed with frustration when he saw a light shining under the door and heard voices. Pressing his ear to the panels, he heard the bishop say, 'Are you sure that hard-bitten bitch cares about her cats?'

'Wouldn't keep them otherwise, now, would she? And the police aren't going to turn out for a couple of cats.'

And then the dean's mocking voice. 'A ransom note?

Man, they'll be combing the place. Did you have a rush of blood to the head or something?'

'Dammit. She'd better pay up or the first furry paw goes out in the post. My mother is going through the books tomorrow with her accountant and I need the shortfall.'

Jimmy retreated along the corridor and thought hard. He was sure if he told them to pay up or he would expose them that the dean would make something nasty happen to him. Agatha would be grateful. He'd tried to be a thief but all that had happened was that he had been caught twice and sentenced to Barlinnie Prison in Glasgow.

He decided to wait until they had gone for the night, rescue the cats, dump them somewhere in that village – Carsely, was it? – and then go back and see if he could rob the office. It all seemed a bit muddled and small-time, but Jimmy knew in his bones, if he tried to fly higher, he always got caught.

He crouched down in an alcove in the corridor until he heard them leave. They seemed to have left the cats behind. At last, when all was silent, he let himself in with a skeleton key after only half an hour of fiddling with the lock. Two pairs of eyes stared up at him from a large cat box. To his relief, the cats were quiet. There was a large safe in the corner. But when did anyone with any money keep it in a safe? He fiddled with the lock on a large desk and opened it up. Under the lid of the desk was a large metal box. He opened it and found it crammed with thousands of pounds. His eyes gleamed.

All he had to do was take the money, get on his motor-bike and head for Spain. What about the cats?

Oh, let them rot! Hodge let out a faint, plaintive miaow. Like a lot of villains, Jimmy was superstitious. If he abandoned the cats, then something really nasty would happen to him. He decided to dump the cats in that village after all. He was consumed with a sudden hatred for the bishop so, although it took some agility, he managed to defecate on the desk and pee all over the leather chair in front of it.

Agatha was asleep, having exhausted herself crying. Mrs Bloxby was asleep as well, an arm around Agatha's shoulders. Voices could be heard coming from outside as more and more people joined in the hunt.

Something woke Mrs Bloxby. She wearily opened her eyes and stared down into Hodge's face. She let out a yelp and poked Agatha hard in the ribs as Boswell joined Hodge.

'Oh, Mrs Raisin. Oh, wake up!'

As the news spread, Agatha's staff came back to watch the two cats tucking into canned mackerel in tomato sauce, one of their favourites.

Now the fun begins, thought Mrs Bloxby, seeing a sudden shadow cross Agatha's face. If I stay much longer, she's going to grill me about Mr Lacey's friend. So, she gave Agatha a final hug and hurried off.

* * *

145

The bishop was in a cold fury as he surveyed the mess of his office. He knew he could not call the police because no matter how much he scrubbed and cleaned, he was sure a forensic team would find a cat hair somewhere.

The dean's voice sounded from behind him. 'We should have left the money for the old folks' home. I mean, all of it, instead of that highly expensive adventure in Thailand. Why didn't you guess the girl was underage?'

'Because the whole damn country seemed to be full of very young girls on offer.'

'Yeah. But you happened to set your sights on a blonde called Sharon from Essex. *And* she was accompanied by that battle-axe of a sister. What came over you? Usually you are content if they run after you, but definitely hands off.'

Bishop Peter gave a bitter laugh. 'What a little actress she was! All that glory of golden hair and sunburnt freckled face. Now we'd better scrub out this filth.'

'It was all your idea. Your filth,' said the dean. 'Mortification is good for the soul.'

Agatha had collapsed into an exhausted sleep on the sofa with the cats sprawled on her lap. When she awoke, everything came flooding back. How exhausting all those police statements had been. But the cats were safe. There was a police guard outside her cottage. So why this black shadow lurking in a corner of her brain?

She sat up suddenly, dislodging the protesting cats. James!

She had meant to find out about that woman but first were all the statements, then she was urged to rest, everyone suddenly deaf to her questions.

Feeling it was all too urgent to get off the sofa and go to the landline, Agatha scrambled in her bag for her mobile phone.

'Why bother?' came Charles's lazy voice from the depths of an armchair by the fire. 'Your marriage to James was lousy, and now you are acting like a dog in the manger.'

'He's awfully stupid when it comes to his choice of women. Remember, he once fell for Toni.'

'Any man would fall for Toni.'

'But not for me.'

'Yes, he did. This is ridiculous. Instead of wondering who nicked your cats, you are working up some soap opera about your ex.'

'Who is she?'

'Leave it.'

'Come on, Charles. Just simple curiosity.'

'Nadia Loncar. Croatian. Works in Cotswold Chic in Mircester. And they are getting married this Saturday.'

'WHAT?! The sneaky bastard never even sent me an invitation.' Overwrought with the adventures of the previous night, Agatha burst into tears.

'Why do I bother?' said Charles to the cats. 'Aggie, shut up and listen. On the left-hand side of your desk is a tray labelled Junk Mail. Now, we all get gold- or silver-embossed invitations to gallery openings and things like that. I bet you just threw it in there without looking. Ah, here it is. See?' He waved it in front of her. Agatha turned her face away.

'Well, watering pot. I'm off. Go to bed and have a proper sleep.'

A transformed Jimmy boarded the Eurostar a month later, wearing a smart charcoal grey suit, white shirt and silk tie. He was clean shaven and his hair was cut short. He had stashed the money in a leather briefcase. If the briefcase had been opened then he would have been in trouble, but he decided to gamble that he would not be searched and the gamble paid off. He was glad he had got the cats back to Agatha. But she couldn't be much of a detective. Look at all those murders and she hadn't even solved one. Bet I'd make a better detective than her any day, he thought. And I'd find out if the bish offed the heiresses.

Agatha was feeling very low indeed. She felt she had been living inside some mad emotional circus. What had happened with Terry? Was it just a matter of chemicals? But it had been the love of legend, of poetry, not like the usual obsessions she fell into.

Autumn was now holding the countryside in its misty fingers and moisture dripped from the thatch of Agatha's cottage. She had bought James a wedding present, gone to his wedding and wished him well, although she could not help envying Nadia's beauty.

She told herself that she had grown up at last. Now, why had she never gone to see Lawrence Crowther, the farmer who had been engaged to Jennifer? Julian had dispensed with her services a good few weeks ago. Agatha had charged him very little, realising for the first time that her mind had not really been on the job. Her reputation had taken a hard blow; in fact, several blows. She had been shown up as the sort of woman who breaks up marriages and was so stupid about her own security that people just seemed to walk into her cottage, murdering people and thieving cats. She now had metal gates across the front and back of her cottage. 'I am the one in prison behind bars,' she muttered.

Agatha summoned her staff and said she meant, although not being paid for it, to try one last time to find Jennifer Toynby, alive or dead.

She selected Toni to help her and allocated the other jobs to the remaining staff. As Agatha drove out of Mircester in the direction of Crowther's farm, she asked Toni, 'Have you ever been in love? I mean like in romances?'

'I've thought so, but I've been lucky so far not to ever have been truly in love. It seems to drive people mad.'

'Give me an example.'

'This girl I used to go to school with, well, she thought she was having Elvis's baby.'

'I am not talking about idiots. I am talking about moon and June and all the poets.'

'Let me think. Will this rain never stop? I thought we were going to have a nice summer.' Silence apart from the sound of the engine and the swish of the windscreen wipers.

'Maybe,' said Toni at last. 'But it was so sad. Girl like me.

'I went to a lousy school. I tried to escape it by getting tough. I went to the library. That took courage. On the way home lads would stop me and snatch my books, jumping up and down on them, while I stood with tears running down my cheeks. Police did nothing. There was just one other girl like me. Then one day, there was this boy waiting for her, holding a bunch of flowers. He approached her. She blushed a bit and then they walked off together. I saw her a few days later and – oh, this is odd – she looked as if she were walking in a golden cloud. She had a look of exalwhatsit?'

'Exultation.'

'Yeah. Creepy. Felt it should be the look of a saint, not some girl who'd just lost her cherry.'

'How do you know she wasn't a virgin?'

'Talk of the boys' toilets at school. Well, she got to hear that he'd bet the others he could screw her. He was a slimy devious bastard and he did the romantic bit pretty well. She couldn't see it. She had been walking on air.'

'I can hardly bear to hear the end of this saga but I suppose she topped herself?'

'It has a happy ending.'

'Get on with you!'

'It's true,' said Toni. 'The star of the football team, Roger McVee, felt sorry for her and began walking her home from school. Next thing he goes and beats the crap out of her seducer. Then she's got a ring on her finger and is the envy of every girl in the school!'

Agatha sighed. 'You made that last bit up.'

'Just for once,' said Toni, 'it would be great to have a happy ending.'

'So, what really happened?'

'Overdose. Pumped out. Life saved. Parents moved to another town. The end. But she really did have her moment of glory. You've never seen anything like that aura she had. You've . . . Oh, forget it. We're nearly there, aren't we?' For Toni had suddenly remembered Agatha's brief fling with Terry.

'Yes.'

'And no one's paying us?'

'Nope. But I have a feeling the bishop pinched my cats.'

'Agatha, whoever killed Terry and whoever stole your cats seems to have been able to get past the burglar alarm system very easily.'

'After Terry, I got the system replaced and again after the cats were stolen.'

'So, it figures that an employee of that company is crooked. The church often has sessions to reform criminals. Do you really think Bishop Peter would go to such lengths?'

'Might. He's a money-grabbing scumbag. Oh, I do hate farms, and farms in the rain mean mud.'

'No mud here,' said Toni. 'Nice tarmacked drive.'

Agatha parked in the farmyard. Her fingers searched nervously for the can of pepper spray she usually kept in her pocket. The door opened and a young man stood looking at her. He was wearing what looked like a caftan, swirls of green and gold. His face was small and triangular and his eyes were pitch black.

'What?' he asked.

Rapidly, Agatha outlined the reason for her visit.

He turned and walked back into the house. After a moment's hesitation, they followed him down a stone-flagged passage and into the kitchen.

'Sit!' he ordered, pointing to some chairs. Outside the rain grew heavier and a sad wind howled in the eaves.

'You are still searching for Jennifer?' he asked after Agatha had explained the reason for her visit.

'Yes.'

'Think I bumped her off?'

'Don't know. Did you?'

'No, but I wouldn't put it past the dean. I asked her why she had broken up with Peter and she said he was only after her money.'

'There have been mentions of some American preacher,' said Agatha.

'I heard those. Everyone seemed to know about it but no one could give me a name or a description. I think she's dead.'

They were seated in the farmhouse kitchen and it did look like a room in a working farmhouse. From her host's appearance, Agatha had expected something more 'interior decorated'. 'Are you really a working farmer?' she asked curiously.

'I could ask if you are really a private detective. Neither of us fits the stereotype.'

'How did you meet Jennifer?'

'At a hunt ball, crying her eyes out in the corner. The bishop wanted a cheque for his old folks' home and her financial advisors told her not to pay until they had gone over the books. So, he refused and she refused and he threw a tantrum and she said the dean threatened to break her legs. I told her to go to the police. Anyway, a week later we were engaged . . .'

'Why?' asked Toni.

Those black eyes looked her up and down. 'Because I fell in lurv, sweetie. That answer your question?'

'No,' said Toni. 'You are not the type to fall in love just like that. I think you are a farmer because of tax benefits and I think you may have looked on Jennifer as another one.'

For a moment there was something almost reptilian in those eyes of his and then he gave a reluctant laugh. 'Something like that.'

'Can you describe her character?' asked Agatha.

'I think she'd been on drugs at one time. *Waiting for Godot* sort of person. Looking for some sort of enlightenment. What she really wanted was a substitute mother or father. Met her parents? Enough to turn anyone's brain.'

'Which one of you broke off the engagement?' asked Agatha, looking longingly at a glass ashtray on the table in front of her and wondering if she dare light up.

'I did. Couldn't stand the weeping bouts or the cling-ing. Perhaps she committed suicide.'

'I think if she had, we'd have found her,' said Agatha. 'Suicides like to be found.'

Toni said, 'Unless she committed suicide at her parents' home.'

'What are you talking about?' asked Agatha. And to their host, 'Mind if I have a cigarette?'

'Yes.'

'Do you mean, yes, you mind, or yes, I can smoke?'

'I mind.'

'It's like this,' said Toni. 'I remember a case in the papers two years ago about a teenager who had hanged herself at her home and left a note blaming the parents. They couldn't bear the idea of the scandal and buried her in the back garden where a neighbour saw them and reported it to the police.'

'We may never know,' he said sententiously. 'You have taken up enough of my time. Good bye.'

'Well, what did you make of him?' asked Agatha, pulling into the nearest pub car park. 'I mean, can you imagine him up at dawn to milk the cows?'

'From where I was sitting,' said Toni, 'I could see through the window into the yard and he employs quite a lot of people. Either he terrifies them or pays high wages but they were so quiet. I mean, I know I was inside and the glass in the window panes was thick but I noticed that they didn't even talk to each other. Which reminds me, I have something to tell you. I'll wait until you have a drink.'

To Agatha's delight, the pub had what they called a 'smoking terrace', which meant tables and chairs sheltered by plastic. She ordered a large gin and tonic and lit up a cigarette.

'Aren't they about eleven pounds a packet now?' asked Toni.

'So what? It's a luxury. I thought you had something to tell me.'

'I wonder if I should. It's about James's marriage.'

'Oh, do tell.'

'I was on a date last night. Bit of a disappointment. Went to the bar at the George. He had seemed a nice fellow but once in the George he became all Hooray Henry, talking loudly and laughing a sort of braying laugh. I said I had to go to the ladies' just to get a break from him. You know, it's off the dining room. I saw James and Nadia. They were seated at a corner table. She looked like a model. You know, black chiffon dress and—'

'I don't care what she was wearing,' said Agatha in a thin voice. 'Get to the point.'

'They weren't speaking to each other.'

'And that's it! Marital tiff, that's all.'

'They looked *bored* with each other.'

'Why the hell did he want to marry her in the first place?'

'She's gorgeous, Agatha.'

'Mark my words, Toni, as the song says, love is a many splendoured thing with a drooping hemline and colours that fade in the wash.'

Toni giggled. 'I don't remember that bit.'

'Oh, well, James is a difficult man.'

'I haven't seen Charles lately.'

Agatha raised her hand and ordered more drinks. 'This is about the longest he's been away. Probably romancing some other heiress.

'Let's talk about the murders,' she continued. 'Now, we can guess why that policeman was murdered. He was about to leak something to the press. Terry was murdered in my cottage, no doubt to try to get me to drop the case. Or it was me they were after and they ran into him. But how did he get in? Someone must have let him in.'

'You've forgotten. Doris's husband let him in.'

'That's right. Okay. Now, let's think. Why Millicent?'

'She must have found something out. And she was always hanging around the bishop. Let's go and ask Mavis,' said Toni.

'They've got steak and kidney pie on the menu,' said Agatha wistfully.

'But we'll feel sluggish afterwards and won't feel like trying to get information out of such as Mavis.'

'All right. I just wish we never had to see that village again.'

'Look, Agatha, she has demonstrated that she is very

jealous of you so all you are going to get is abuse. Let me see her alone.'

While Agatha sat puffing on a cigarette in the car, Toni tried the manor house. Getting no reply, she made her way to the church.

Agatha and her detectives had become accustomed to Toni's beautiful fair hair, blue eyes and a perfect figure, but to Mavis, hearing a sound behind her and turning around, it was like some sort of visitation. A rare gleam of sunlight was shining down through a stained-glass window onto the long, white, cotton dress Toni was wearing. But as Mavis was about to sink to her knees, the church grew dark again and she realised angels did not carry handbags.

'Have you come to see the church?' she demanded. 'I am sure I have seen you before.'

For some reason, Toni decided not to mention she was a detective. 'I was here at the bishop's visit,' she said.

'Ah, my very dear bishop.' Mavis moved closer up the aisle, her sturdy brogues making hardly any sound as she moved so slowly. 'We are to be married, you know.'

'Was the announcement in the newspapers?'

'Oh, no. Too many jealous women. And I am not only doing it for me, but for my poor, dead sister.' She suddenly gave Toni a sly look and then solemnly winked. 'Also, I know who the murderer is.'

'And who is that?'

Mavis's voice dropped to a whisper. 'I'll tell you after the wedding.'

Although the day was warm and humid, Toni felt the hairs rise on her arms. Mavis was quite close now. She looked somehow lit up from within. 'I will be marrying a good man. He will make the announcement of our betrothal on Saturday.'

'What happens on Saturday?'

'It is the official opening of the bishop's old folks' home.'

'Some personalities can give you claustrophobia.' Toni remembered Agatha saying that once. Whatever it was that Mavis was emanating was making Toni feel nauseated. She gave a jerky little nod of the head and fled the church.

Chapter Eight

When Mrs Bloxby phoned to invite Agatha to the opening of the old folks' home, Agatha was tempted to refuse. She had begun to look forward to her days off and once more toyed with the idea of turning the agency over to Toni. And yet, somewhere, in a file in her brain marked Unfinished Business, lay all the notes she had made on the murders.

Also the bishop's mother was to attend after visiting Thirk Magna first and Agatha was curious to see her with the bishop.

On Saturday morning, as she dressed, she heard the sound of the bells of Thirk Magna sounding across the wolds. She could see them all in her mind's eye: Mavis Dupin, Helen Toms, Harry Bury, Julian Brody, Colin Docherty, Joseph Merrydown and Gloria Buxton. What an odd assortment!

As Mrs Bloxby got into Agatha's car, Agatha said, 'Tell me again about bell ringing. Are the people who go in for it all crazy?'

'It's such a mathematical pastime, like chess,' said the vicar's wife, 'so usually very sensible people take it up.

Of course, there have been Sunday supplement articles recently about how it is good for the figure. That probably was the initial attraction for Mrs Gloria Buxton, although her desire to become the lawyer's wife soon took over. Of course, Mr Brody will be losing interest in Mrs Toms and will be out there looking for someone else to save. I seriously doubt if he will ever save anyone because he does not like to be committed, you see.'

'Are you usually so cynical?'

'One gets that way being a vicar's wife. I am an unpaid counsellor. In my opinion someone mad has committed these murders and I think it was the same person who did them all. I think they all knew something that the murderer was frightened they would talk about.'

'Here's buggering gawdawful Thirk sodding bejesus Magna again,' said Agatha and burst into tears.

Mrs Bloxby put an arm round Agatha's shoulders, feeling awkward because one did not really hug someone such as Agatha Raisin. 'It is grief,' said the vicar's wife.

Agatha finally dried her eyes. 'How can I grieve over such a sordid little affair?'

'But it was the power and glory while it lasted,' said Mrs Bloxby sadly. 'We can go home if you like? I did not say this before because of the upset in your life but I feel I must say it now. It is your Christian duty to use all your talents to find this killer.'

'I'll try.'

'And as you wiped away your tears with a dirty rag,

you had better take one of my face cleansers and repair your makeup.'

Agatha reached in the backseat and heaved a large bag full of cosmetics over. Mrs Bloxby was glad they had arrived early because it took Agatha twenty minutes to do her makeup to her satisfaction.

She got out of the car and peered up at the sky. 'Looks like rain.'

Black mountains of cloud were swirling up against a grey sky. Agatha turned and saw an old Bentley car heading for the vicarage. Helen Toms was out on the front step, curtsying as if before royalty as the tall, thin figure of Lady Fathering descended from her car and towered over her. Behind her came her husband with a creepy smile. Her ladyship inclined her head and said something, and the Tomses got into her limo.

'So, what did you think of her?' asked Mrs Bloxby as they followed the limo out onto the Mircester road.

'Tall, tweedy, cold. Hardly the type to want a baby.'

'We'll see. There's some sort of reception. You will probably get to meet her if you push.'

Agatha looked surprised. 'I *never* push.'

Goodness. She actually believes that, thought Mrs Bloxby.

The bell ringers were out in force. Helen Toms had been relegated to their ranks so that her place could be taken at the bishop's side by Mavis Dupin.

In seats along the wall were the elderly new residents of the brand-new home.

'I am going to have a look around,' whispered Agatha.

161

'But the speeches are about to begin!'

'Then it's a good time to go.'

Agatha quietly left the room and made her way along a corridor, stone-flagged and musty. Where were the offices? As if in answer to her unspoken question, there was a board when she rounded the corridor with signs TO OFFICE, TO CHAPEL, TO TOILETS, TO KITCHEN and so on.

She located the office and tried the handle. To her surprise the door was not locked.

She let herself in and jumped in alarm as the dean's voice demanded, 'Looking for something, Mrs Raisin?'

'Sorry. Need the loo.'

'It is quite clearly signposted. I think you are snooping and I don't like snoops.'

Agatha was about to retreat when her eyes focussed on his white robe. A few cat hairs were clinging to it. She was about to accuse him but quickly decided that would be too dangerous so she gave him an apologetic smile and quickly made her way back down the corridor.

As she entered the room, Lady Fathering was in full flow. She broke off and glared at Agatha.

'Is there a policeman in the house?' asked Agatha.

Bill Wong made his way from the back of the room. Agatha whispered urgently that the dean had cat hair on his robe. Bill signalled to a policeman and together hurried off.

'Have you quite finished?' demanded Lady Fathering. Agatha snapped, 'Yes,' her eyes on the door, hoping the dean hadn't discovered the hairs and brushed them off. But she was aware of the bishop's eyes searching her face.

'As I was saying,' boomed Lady Fathering, 'the bishop has worked tirelessly to raise money to give these ladies shelter in their declining years. The new building is at the other side of the cloisters. I suggest you all follow me there.'

But the door opened and Bill Wong and the policeman entered, each one holding the dean by the arm.

Bishop Peter turned quite white. 'What on earth is going on?' he demanded.

'I am being charged with nicking the Raisin woman's cats. Get the lawyer.'

'We need you at headquarters as well,' said Bill to the bishop.

'I will follow you there,' said Peter haughtily, 'after I have opened the old folks' home.'

It was a long day with the bishop making an extremely tedious speech.

'This will make headlines,' whispered Mrs Bloxby.

'Only if found guilty,' said Agatha. 'They'll put the blame on someone or get one of these infatuated women to confess. I'm quite hungry. I thought there would be some sort of buffet. Let's call in at the Greek place and talk to that Glaswegian. He might have some clues.'

Not only had the Greek restaurant been transformed

into a curry house, but they learned that Jimmy had just left one day and they hadn't heard from him since.

'Maybe there'll be something in the newspapers,' said Mrs Bloxby. 'All the locals were there and they followed the police and then ran out of the room.'

'Oh look,' said Agatha, 'that tea shop over there is new. Let's comfort ourselves with pots of tea and cream cakes.

'The sad fact is,' said Agatha half an hour later, 'bad weather plays hell with the waistline. That's when I want comfort food. You know, I can hardly say I have had one intuitive breakthrough.'

'What exactly do you mean by intuitive?'

'It is like this. I am like a Victorian detective. I do not have access to forensics or autopsy reports so I have to rely on old-fashioned intuition and guesswork. Also, I haven't been asking enough questions. I shy away from the murder of Terry. I feel guilty, so I don't stop to ask, what made him a threat? And although Doris's husband let him in, how did the killer get in?'

'Over the garden fence? Perhaps the garden door was left open to let the cats out.'

'James might have seen something. Finished? I'll pay for this and then we'll go and see James.'

'I'm afraid I cannot accompany you. Parish work.'

'I'll drop you off.'

Agatha, after she had left Mrs Bloxby, walked next door to James's cottage and banged on the door.

It was opened by Nadia carrying a suitcase. 'Off on holiday?' asked Agatha.

'I am going home,' she said.

'James?'

'Inside.'

Agatha walked into the living room. A log fire was burning and James was seated in an armchair in front of it.

His face was set in hard lines. 'Did I come at the wrong moment?' asked Agatha.

'You are one walking, talking wrong moment,' said James. 'Oh, sit down. Nadia has left me.'

'What did you do?' asked Agatha. 'Tell her to wear flat heels and no makeup?'

'I wanted to shake it out of her,' he said sadly.

'What?'

'Love. I couldn't believe it had gone, just like that. I had never experienced anything like it before. In fact, I thought it didn't exist. I think it was Aristophanes, interpreting Plato, who claimed that once we were all androgynous, and that one day we were all cut in half and doomed to search the world for our lost half. It was like that. Utter madness. I think the chemicals in our brains or body trick us and I wonder if what I briefly experienced was not love but the total end to loneliness. Self-sufficient people like me never think of themselves as being lonely but I suppose deep down every human being is just that. Anyway, I was locked with her in a golden bubble and nothing in the outside world could spoil or get near that glory.

'It is like some awful Greek myth. I woke up one morning and there she was, a beautiful but not very intelligent Croatian.'

'I felt like that with Terry,' said Agatha. 'I was prepared to throw everything up, ruin his marriage, give up my career and go to Australia. People should be warned against it, like manic depression or psychosis. At least I'll know what it really is the next time.'

'I'll make some coffee,' said James.

Agatha sat and stared into the flames, feeling somewhat comforted that she had found someone who could explain that recent madness.

James returned and handed her a mug of coffee and a large ashtray. 'I am even going to allow you to smoke,' he said. 'But aren't you ashamed to be so old-fashioned?'

'Bollocks!'

'Still, alcohol will follow now they have put the price up in Scotland.'

'Bollocks to that, too. I read an article once about how people got their highs before they could afford decent booze. Cider with surgical spirit, Coca-Cola and two codeine, or make your own with wood alcohol and go blind. But you have said something so important I have to think. Shut up for a moment.'

Agatha lit a cigarette, reflecting that James must be really upset to allow her to smoke.

If she herself had temporarily gone mad, what about one of the suspects? The bishop had been working on so many women to fund that nursing home. Why? She could swear he hadn't an altruistic bone in his body. She could also swear that the bishop had a definite feminine side.

That might have explained his desire for gorgeous robes and getting up in the pulpit. In was indeed a wonder that with looks like his, he hadn't gone on the stage. She voiced this last thought aloud.

'I think his mother controls him along with the purse strings. I think his friendship with the dean is close because the dean finds ways to get round the mother's possible parsimony.

'I need someone to talk to the bishop's mother,' said Agatha.

'Don't look at me. You need someone like Charles. In fact, someone just drove past.'

James went to his front door and looked out. Then Agatha heard him call, 'Charles! In here.'

Agatha realised that she had not talked to Charles for a good few weeks.

'That coffee smells nice,' said Charles. 'Any chance of a cup and I'll just have one of your cigarettes.'

'Not unless you promise to do something for me.'

'Like what?'

'Go to Lady Fathering and find out why her son so desperately wanted this old folks' home.'

'And what do I get in return?'

'You may have a cigarette and here is James with your coffee. What more do you need?'

'Oh, thanks, James. Where is Nadia?'

'Gone.'

'Ouch. Want to talk about it?'
'No. Not now.'

To Agatha's surprise, Charles called on her two evenings later to say that he had visited Lady Fathering.

'Get me a stiff drink and a cigarette at the double. Goodness, that woman has had a maternal bypass,' said Charles.

Agatha waited impatiently until Charles, with cigarette in one hand and a double whisky in the other said, 'In her late husband's will, he would only leave her all the wealth if it could be shown that she had made provisions for his three maiden aunts to be looked after. He died in his sixties. Aunties are all pushing ninety. Think of the expense! So, she orders her son to look after them so that she can claim that she has made provisions for them. If not, she will disinherit him.

'Could not help asking why she had adopted him in the first place. I gather it was to help a friend, I said. She said, no. Actually, it was because Diana "Boofuls" Teddington was swanning around with her brat and our lady here could not bear the competition. Now Peter did not want to be a bishop, but she insisted. Also, that he took one of the family names of Salver-Hinkley. The latest is that all those ladies the bish had been romancing to get into their bank accounts have found him growing cold. Hey, what about the cat hair?'

'Being tested. Dean says it is the chapel cat. But he had a nasty gloating look on his face. I bet he got rid of those cat hairs the minute I had gone, got the chapel moggy and rubbed it all over his cassock. Charles, have you any idea who might have committed these murders?'

'My money is on Helen Toms. I think she fell for the bishop because there was no hope there but she didn't know that. And she is the kind to be unobtainable. The next one to go will be her husband.'

'Too obvious.'

'Might be biding her time. Might be working on Julian.'

'Don't think so. Julian probably has moved on to look for another married woman he can rescue. Anyway, Bill Wong told me that the wicked Lady Fathering is off to the south of France. So, I'll bet you anything, the bishop and his dean head off on holiday as well but far away from the south of France. What do you know about Plato or Aristhistonics, or whatever his name was?'

'Not a lot. Oh, you're talking about the other half?'

'Yes.'

'You never cease to amaze me.' Charles's eyes sharpened. 'Terry. Bless my heart and may it never stop. So, you thought you had found your other half?'

'I didn't. Something stupid in the chemicals in my body did.'

'So where is this leading?'

'Say some woman felt this for the bishop. It might drive her to murder.'

'I think for it to work, he'd need to feel the same.'

'He can switch emotion on and off like a tap. I think

he'll have to wait around until he is cleared of stealing my cats.'

'Be careful,' said Charles. 'If it's not a woman but the bishop himself who is our murderer, he might decide to silence you. And forget about this Plato business if you are looking for an excuse to explain why you were ready to destroy someone's marriage.'

'If you were a woman, Charles, you would be called a bitch. How do you think I solved previous cases?'

'By bumbling about and putting yourself at risk until the murderer comes after you. Elementary, my dear Watson.'

'Yes, but to tempt the real murderer, I have to know who the murderer is. See, smarty pants?'

'Yes, but you don't know in this case. While you are dropping hints, *clang, clang, clang*, in front of our bishop, the real murderer, say Helen Toms, creeps up behind you with an axe.'

'Trolley.'

'What trolley? Are you off yours?'

'Judy Garland. Clang, clang, clang went the trolley. As you were being sarcastic about me dropping hints, you should have said clunk, clunk, clunk. Anyway, get this, I am going to stage something.'

'What, now?' said Charles. 'Ladies and gentlemen, please be seated in the library. I will shortly unmask the murderer. That sort of thing?'

'So what? I will phone the newspapers.'

'Who are you going to accuse? Agatha! You are as daft as a brush.'

'Ah, this is the clever bit. I tell everyone I know the identity of the murderer and I have just a few loose ends to tie up.'

'Like the loose wiring in your brain. I'm off, Agatha. No, not another word. It's all mad. And don't give me any more of that Aristophanes crap. You had a grubby little affair without any thought for anyone else.'

'Like who, Charles?' Agatha asked quietly. But the slamming of the door was her only answer.

After he had left, Agatha began to feel almost as stupid as Charles obviously thought she was. Nobody was paying her to find out the identity of the murderer. She needed to take the staff off their present cases and set them all to work by . . . how?

After some hard thought, Agatha phoned Toni and asked her to take charge of the work in the office in the morning. 'I must find out who this murderer is,' explained Agatha. 'He's broken into my house and, if it is the bishop as I am sure it is, he even dared to pinch my cats.'

At the other end of the line, Toni reflected Agatha must be well and truly over Terry in that she should consider the kidnapping of her cats as a more serious crime than the death of her lover.

After she had rung off, Agatha decided to go back to Thirk Magna in the morning and begin with the bell ringers.

* * *

The next morning was a typical late autumn day with mist shrouding the wolds and hanging crystals of moisture from the bushes. The bells were ringing. She was sure the noise was based on some mathematical set of changes but to her, she had to admit, it was nothing more than a jumble of sound. She suddenly wondered who had replaced Millicent.

Unfriendly eyes stared at her as she entered the bell chamber. There was a newcomer she had not met before, a tall, thin man with thick glasses and a long head that looked as if it had been squashed at birth.

'If it ain't our very own Miss Marple,' jeered Harry Bury, the sexton.

'I was about to offer to buy you all drinks over at the pub,' said Agatha. 'But if that's your attitude, you can . . .'

Harry thought quickly of his low wages. Drinks with Agatha meant he might be able to have a Scotch along with a pint of beer. 'Just joking,' he said hurriedly. 'Right kind, I'm sure.' The others mumbled their acceptance.

Julian fell into step beside Agatha as they all walked to the pub. 'Now, what are you up to?' he asked.

'I'll tell you when you are all listening. Who's the newcomer?'

'Oh, Sydney Carton. Yes, that was fortuitous. And I've heard all the jokes about "It is a far, far better thing I do . . ." and I suppose he has, too.'

'What are you talking about?'

'That book by Charles Dickens. You know, the one about the French Revolution.'

'Yes, now I know what you are talking about,' lied Agatha, who really still hadn't a clue but was used to covering up the vast gulfs in her education.

'Fortuitous? You mean, he's a newcomer and he happened to be a bell ringer as well?'

'Yes.'

In the pub, Agatha took their orders and passed them to the barman who said he would carry the drinks over to their table. After Agatha was seated, she glanced under the table at Sydney's shoes. They were black and highly polished. She wondered whether he was an undercover policeman. The press had recently begun to goad the police again about all the unsolved murders.

He introduced himself as a retired civil servant who was on a walking tour and had learned they needed a bell ringer and he was passionate about campanology.

A Tale of Two Cities, thought Agatha suddenly. Her mother had once dumped her at the local church hall while she went to the pub because there was an old movie showing. It had been black-and-white with Ronald Colman playing Sydney Carton. Is he under-cover? Stupid to take such an alias. Drawn attention. The drinks were served. Mumbles of thanks all round.

Julian was seated next to Gloria Buxton. Agatha noticed that Helen Toms did not look at all pleased. The butcher, Joseph Merrydown, said, 'And what brings you back, Mrs Raisin?'

'To let you all know that I have found out the identity of the murderer and will make an announcement tomorrow.'

There was a sudden silence. The pub was an old-fashioned country one with worn linoleum on the floor and whitewashed walls, stained with nicotine from the days before the smoking ban.

Then Sydney said, 'You are nothing more than a publicity seeker. Miss Dupin here lost her sister and now you are opening old wounds. Shame on you!'

'I am not a publicity seeker. I am a murderer seeker,' said Agatha.

'So, where's the big announcement to be made?' asked Julian.

Agatha thought quickly. 'In the church hall in Carsely.'

Helen Toms looked doubtful. 'I am surprised to hear that the Bloxbys are letting you have the use of the hall. It is the rehearsal night for *Whither Britannia?*'

'Never heard of it,' said Agatha.

Helen gave a patronising little giggle. 'You should know what goes on in your own village. Mr Carton here says we are forgetting how to be British and he has prepared tunes and songs to give a patriotic feel.'

Agatha scowled. She did not want to offend Mrs Bloxby, who handled all the bookings for the church hall.

'Why not have it in the church hall here?' said Gloria. 'I, for one, will be there to see you make a right fool of yourself. I don't for one moment believe you know who it is. And why won't you tell us now?'

'I want the press there so that the whole of Britain will be on the lookout for him.'

'Well, you're not getting the hall here,' said Helen.

Agatha took out her phone and dialled a number. 'Ah, vicar,' Helen heard her say. 'May I rent the church hall here from you for tomorrow morning? Good. That's settled.'

Agatha rang off and gave a wide smile across the table at Helen. 'Easy-peasy. Nothing to worry about.'

Colin Docherty said in his high reedy voice, 'Aren't you forgetting one thing? That the killer may kill you tonight to shut you up?'

'By this time, he will think I know nothing,' said Agatha.

'Why?' asked Mavis.

'He's had a lot of time to paste over the cracks.'

Agatha, as soon as she got home, began to phone round all the newspapers, news agencies and television channels. Then she took her cats round to Doris, returned home, packed a suitcase and checked in at a Premier Inn outside Mircester on the ring road.

It was then that she wondered uneasily if she had found a new way of committing suicide. She now thought of Terry as 'an unfortunate episode', no longer wanting to dignify the experience with the name of love. It had begun to rain and the passing traffic made swishing sounds, coming and going through the dark night.

She tried to be philosophical. 'I've had a good life,' she said to the uncaring walls.

Then she found herself thinking rebelliously that her life had been nothing but easy. And why did it always feel a bit empty if there wasn't a man around? The new woman was surely supposed to be self-sufficient. I suppose she could be, thought Agatha, if her hormones had been surgically removed. It was then she realised with a jolt that she had booked the room under her own name. Better change the hotel. But comfort food first.

She walked through to the restaurant attached. One window was opened because it was an unusually warm November, if damp. 'Have you ordered yet?' asked a voice behind her.

'Give me a chance,' grumbled Agatha. 'I just got here.'

She studied the menu and did not see the hand that went into her handbag on a chair beside her or remove her car keys. Nor did she notice as the key fob was clicked at the window, opening her car parked outside.

Charles elbowed his way into the church hall at Thirk Magna the following day. He could not find a free seat but propped himself up against the wall, next to the platform. Agatha had declared she would make her announcement at eleven o'clock in the morning. Eleven came and went. No Agatha.

'Silly cow,' came a masculine voice in the hall. 'Just another publicity hunter who knows bugger all.'

There was a rumble of agreement. Charles began to

worry. Agatha would not have run away from the situation. She would have turned up and either waffled her way out of it, or, although he doubted it, she now had a good idea as to the identity of the murderer. He knew that she often, in a way, forced herself into a mental corner and that was sometimes when that acute intuition of hers took over. Perhaps this was one of the times it hadn't worked. But she still would have shown up. Where the hell was she? He scrambled up onto the platform and surveyed the room. Who was missing? All the bell ringers were there. What about the dean and the bishop?

He went outside and saw Agatha's small staff huddled together. Toni ran to meet him. 'We didn't know about this until I heard it on the radio yesterday. She hasn't contacted us. I phoned the bishop and got the dean. The pair of them are over at Whiton opening a sale of work and they stayed at the hotel there last night and no one saw them leave. Locals swear they never left the hotel.'

'I phoned round all the hotels,' said Phil Marshall. 'She booked into a Premier Inn out on the ring road under her own name. But when I rang she had gone to bed.'

'What came over her to make such an amateur mistake?' raged Charles.

'But she wanted to be found,' Simon pointed out.

'In the hall and on her own terms,' said Toni. 'Where is she?'

* * *

Agatha recovered consciousness. It was pitch black. Her head throbbed and there was a crust of something over most of her face. Bits of things were stabbing into her back. She tried to cry for help, but her voice was a weak croak and she fell unconscious again.

When she recovered once more, her chest was heaving, trying to get air. There was a little chink of light to the right. Although her arms were folded across her chest, she found she had some wiggle room. Agatha remembered she had a pen in her inside pocket and after a lot of wiggling, got it out. She managed to get the pen inside the hole and screwed round and around it until she felt some air coming in.

Agatha opened her mouth to call for help and then decided against it. If the murderer were out there, then he or she might finish the job. And as bits of memory came back in flashes, Agatha realised that the murderer had probably thought her dead when she had been put in this hole. Think! She remembered getting in her car, surprised to find out that she had apparently not locked it. Then pain and darkness.

Mrs Bloxby would urge her to pray. It wasn't that Agatha never prayed; it was more that her prayers consisted of doing deals with God – 'Get me out of this, God, and I will never smoke again' type of thing.

But for some reason, she found herself begging the Almighty to look after her friends and see that Toni found a decent man if she ever got married. Then she lay very still and prepared to welcome death.

But a little flicker of sunlight glinted at the airhole and she heard a voice intone, 'Man that is born of a woman hath but a short time to live, and is full of misery. He cometh up and is cut down like a flower; he fleeth as it were a shadow, and never continueth in one stay.'

The burial service, thought Agatha. They don't know I am not dead. Let me think. That bit is said at the graveside which we all know, thanks to the telly rather than church attendance. Oh, damn it to hell. They'd all have been in here beforehand because I must be somewhere in the church but at ground level or I wouldn't have heard the service coming in from the grave. I can't accept death any more.

But she blacked out again.

She came to some hours later and realised there were a lot of footsteps above her and that the church was filling up. She tried shouting but her voice was dry and weak and the organ was playing.

Then she heard the voice of the vicar, 'We are gathered here together to pray for Agatha Raisin. And so we have this special evening service requested by her friends to send her hope and courage if she is still alive. So please be upstanding and join together in the twenty-third psalm.'

It was during the singing of the psalm that Agatha remembered her cigarettes and lighter were in the inside pocket of her jacket. She wriggled her hand into the pocket.

The movement of her body caused again a crunching sound from underneath her. Agatha realised it was probably an old, old skeleton that she was grinding into bone meal.

She found the packet and dragged it out. Then it seemed to take forever to find that lighter.

Charles sat at the end of a pew feeling bleak and lost. The Reverend Toms's voice rose in the evening prayer. '"O praise the Lord for it is a good thing to sing praises unto our God; yea, a joyful and pleasant thing it is to be thankful. The Lord doth build up Jerusalem: and gather together the outcasts of Israel. He helpeth those that are broken in heart, and giveth medicine to heal their sickness."'

Maybe we should have got married, he thought. But husband or not, I cannot see Agatha letting me stop her behaving like this.

'"He telleth the number of the stars and ..." Well, really! This is too bad. Smoking in church and on such a solemn occasion.'

Charles stood up and looked wildly round. James, who was in another pew, came to join him.

'Look!' he said.

From a hole in a slab of gravestone on the floor of the aisle of the church a pathetic little smoke ring wavered up.

Chapter Nine

'Get a crowbar!' yelled Charles. 'I think she's under here.'

'Here's one,' said the sexton. 'Hang on. I'll get another.'

'I beg you to go carefully,' admonished the vicar. 'That is the grave of Abigail Torine, buried in 1722. Such a pretty poem and so apt.

> "Done with workin
> Gone to God
> Don't forget
> To feed the dog."

'Quite moving, is it not?'

'Oh, shut the hell up,' shouted Charles. 'Ah, right now. Don't want to drop it back on her.'

Harry put his crowbar on one side and James on the other. Patrick and Simon waited until the stone was raised up a bit and put their hands under it to balance it. They tipped it away. It fell against a pew with a crash and broke into three pieces.

Smiling up at them through a mask of crusted blood

was Agatha. 'Stay where you are,' ordered James. 'Let the paramedics move you.'

'No, I've got to look at who's here. I'll bet the beast who did this to me is hanging around.'

Despite their protests, she eventually was supported out of the grave and looked around the congregation. Love, she thought. Crazy love. Aristowhatsit. Him. Whole thing with Terry was mad. The bishop is here and the dean. The dean for the bishop. Julian for Helen. Oh, my goodness.

'It's Mavis Dupin,' she shouted before losing consciousness again.

Chapter Ten

Agatha was put into an induced coma in the hospital while her head was operated on. Her friends came and went. James was getting fed up with Roy Silver. In his emotional gratitude at finding Agatha alive, he had offered Roy a room in his house. And Roy always seemed to appear looking camper than ever if some of James's old army friends called.

On one such visit, a retired general had put his hand on James's knee, winked and said, 'We must get together soon.'

At last when Agatha was out of her coma, he got her keys to give to Roy, only to find that Roy had packed up and left for London.

'What happened after I accused Mavis?' asked Agatha.

'Nothing.'

'What?'

'Proof, Agatha. Proof. Not a smidgeon.'

'So, the police are calling me a fool,' said Agatha bitterly.

'Strangely enough, they aren't. Although they are looking at all the bell ringers. It was someone who knew the church intimately. Unless it was someone very strong, no one else would think of lifting that gravestone, but someone who knew the history of the church would know that the marble slab was quite thin. But there's all sorts of electrical lifting equipment these days. Also, because of funerals, once the double doors to the main entrance are opened, anyone could drive a vehicle in.'

'Did they check the Premier Inn for security cameras? Surely whoever was after me arrived by car.'

'Quietest part of the year. But they got a brief shot of someone on a bike. You were attacked in your own car by someone hiding in the back and it is possible to get into your car if crouched down and out of sight of the cameras. Why Mavis?'

'I think Bishop Peter drove her mad. He was desperate for money and he can switch on sexuality. Millicent was competing with her on every occasion so Millicent had to go. Larry was selling secrets to the newspapers. Off with him as well. I think she came to get me and found Terry. Maybe jealousy of me made her say things she shouldn't have and so Terry got it.'

'Agatha, there is no police guard on your door so we have organised our own guard. Charles should be here soon.'

'I am sure I can look after myself.'

'Getting buried in an old grave is not exactly what I would call looking after yourself, Agatha. Was it the madness of love that got you on to Mavis?'

'Something like that. You know, when the bishop got

engaged to Ducksy, it's a wonder Mavis didn't murder her as well. Oh, maybe she has. James, I see some angel has brought my makeup bag. Pass it over.'

'You don't want to be looking in a mirror this evening, Agatha. Wait until your hair grows back.'

'What! I want a mirror now, *pullease*.'

'Don't say I didn't warn you.'

Agatha fumbled in her large makeup bag until she found a mirror and held it up. She let out a squawk of dismay. Three quarters of her hair had been shaved off. And on the bald bit were two holes where they had drilled into her head to stop the swelling.

'I look like a bowling ball,' mourned Agatha. 'James, that small case of mine over there might have a scarf in it.'

James looked amused as the transformation began.

Soon she had a green-and-gold chiffon scarf cleverly wound round her head and her face made up.

Charles arrived carrying a bottle of champagne in an ice bucket. 'I don't think she's allowed to drink,' cautioned James.

'More for me. Push off anyway, James. I've only two glasses.'

'Simon will relieve you in two hours,' said James, consulting a list, 'and Patrick is doing the late shift.'

Agatha began to sob. 'You are all so good that . . .'

'Oh, stop bubbling and gabbling,' snapped Charles, shoving a glass of champagne under Agatha's nose.

'I'm off,' said James.

'Anyway, I want to hear all about it,' said Charles.

'Before they induced the coma, the police were here, making me go over everything again and again and making me feel like a fool. And that newcomer, Sydney Carton? That really is his name.'

As Agatha talked Charles drank most of the champagne, and when Agatha fell asleep abruptly, he put away the bottle and glasses, used her shower and towels and, naked, got into the bed with her, cuddled up and fell asleep.

Simon walked into the room later and decided it was all too embarrassing and retreated to a chair in the corridor. A nurse came along and stopped short at the sight of him. She had been briefed on the subject of Agatha's guard.

'You don't need to sit out here,' she said after checking Simon's identity. 'You can go in.'

'Mrs Raisin is otherwise engaged.'

'Oh, that must be Mr Butler, the neurosurgeon. I will just take a look.' And before Simon could stop her, she had opened the door and walked in.

She rapidly came out again, her colour high. 'Well, really! I never did!' she exclaimed.

'Maybe it's time you did,' said Simon to her retreating outraged back.

As Simon expected, she was soon back with the neurosurgeon. Mr Butler shook Charles awake and hissed, 'Could you not have waited? This woman is in no condition to have sex.'

Simon half-listened to the argument going on inside before picking up the paperback he had been reading.

The surgeon and nurse emerged. 'You must understand, those sort of people have no morals,' said Mr Butler.

Patrick turned up at that moment. 'Anything happening?' he asked.

'Charles scandalising everyone by getting off his kit and climbing into bed with Agatha. I gather he just fell asleep but the hospital thought otherwise. Don't go in yet. Sounds like an argy-bargy in there.'

Charles had started it by saying, 'You must stop this business about intuition and try to do some detective work.'

'What the hell are you talking about?'

'The day before you got buried, Toni had found out that Mavis Dupin had spent some months in a psychiatric ward fifteen years ago for torturing the two family dogs to death. It was a private nursing home and she was registered under a false name. But by plodding detective work, Toni found this out and was going to slip you that information before you made a prat of yourself at the village hall.'

'Oh, shut up!' yelled Agatha.

At that moment, Helen Toms walked into the room, carrying a bunch of flowers. 'Now, now,' she admonished them. 'Birds in their little nests agree.'

'Oh, piss off,' said Agatha.

'Must you be so rude?' raged Charles. 'Come along, Helen. Let's leave this silly bitch and go and have a drink.'

'How kind of you, Sir Charles.'

What is up with everyone, thought Agatha tearfully. It is a miracle I am alive and yet no one is being kind to me and Charles hates me.

'I heard you,' said Patrick from the doorway. 'You were really nasty to that woman. Can I get you anything?'

'I feel I could murder a hamburger and fries.'

'There's a place across from the hospital. Back in a tick.'

Patrick soon returned with hamburgers and fries for himself and Agatha and a bottle of red wine. 'Never, *ever* drink white wine with hamburgers,' said Patrick in a mincing voice, making Agatha laugh. 'Mind if I watch your telly? Lewis is on.'

'Help yourself. It's a pity Colin Dexter killed off Morse.'

'Lewis isn't bad. Shhh.'

Patrick settled down happily to watch Lewis solve the mystery of a dead don.

Agatha was suddenly overcome with a feeling of fear and horror. All memories of her incarceration in that tomb came roaring back.

'Patrick! I'm scared,' she shouted.

Patrick picked up the chair he had been sitting on and carried it back to beside the bed.

'Yes, you would be,' said Patrick. 'We should have guessed it was someone who knew that church well. You see, for a small woman like Mavis, she would need to know that the grave she dumped you in had a top that she could lift. The sexton said he thought there was something about that in the church records. The family weren't all that well off and, marble being expensive, they got it cut thin.'

'What did she die of?'

'Typhoid.'

'Hope the germs died with her.'

'Bound to. Try to have a sleep.'

But although Agatha closed her eyes, she found she could not sleep. Instead, she found herself suddenly deciding to turn the agency over to Toni. Then what? Well, it would be nice to settle down with the slippers-in-front-of-the-fire type of marriage. No mad passion. Comfort and companionship. Perhaps she should marry Charles.

But if she really wanted to marry Charles, *she* would need to propose to *him* and he would expect a healthy amount of money from her. Also, she did not want to live at Barfield House with his aunt and Gustav. Perhaps she could keep her cottage and they could come and go from each other's houses. Patrick was asleep in front of the television. A quiz show was on with a hysterical compere, all piano teeth and false hairpiece. Agatha noticed with some irritation that Patrick had fallen asleep clutching the television control. She climbed out of bed and tried to get it out of his hand. He awoke and gave her a vicious backhander that knocked her to the floor.

'I'm sorry,' he gasped. 'I thought we were being attacked. Did you hit your head?'

'No. Just my hip. Help me up.'

Settled once more in bed, Agatha clicked through the

189

channels until she found an old black-and-white movie, *The Lavender Hill Mob*.

'I am sure it would be all right for you to go home, Patrick,' said Agatha. 'I've got this panic button.'

Patrick hesitated. He had a new lady friend, middle-aged like himself. He was beginning to think of marriage. 'If you're sure,' he said.

'Sure as sure. Run along.'

Charles had been out in Mircester to meet an old friend for a drink. He was making his way to the car park when he noticed Patrick strolling along with a buxom matron on his arm.

He waylaid the couple. 'Patrick, aren't you supposed to be guarding Agatha?'

'She said there was no need. She's got the panic button,' protested Patrick.

Charles swung round and raced to his car, jumped in and drove as fast as he could to the hospital.

Agatha was dreaming that she was under the church floor and trying to get air, straining her mouth towards that little air hole. But it all went black and became more suffocating. She opened her eyes to realise the nightmare was real. Someone was pressing something down on her face.

Running footsteps in the corridor. Agatha was released, gulping for air. A black-clad figure ran from the room. She pressed the panic button and nothing happened.

Charles came rushing in followed by the hospital security guard.

'Was it her?'

'I think so. Oh, she cut the wire to my panic button.'

'Phone the police. I'll get to the car park and see if I can find her.'

A search went throughout the night but there was no sign of Mavis Dupin. 'What I cannot understand,' said Charles, 'is why she ran for it after you had been found. The police had nothing against her.'

'I think she was afraid I had recognised her. Charles, I want to get out of here. I'd be safer in my own home. I've got a good security system.'

'Which the killer bypassed before.'

'No, I don't think so. All Mavis had to do was ring the bell. Terry would answer the door. She would say she wanted to wait for me. Once inside, she biffed him. I also think when she slogged me with that hammer that she thought I was dead.'

It was late afternoon by the time Agatha had gained permission to go home. She phoned Doris and begged her to look after the cats for a little longer. Then Charles said he must go to his own home. But he phoned Agatha's office before he left and asked Toni to come and 'babysit this walking disaster'.

Toni's first words were, 'Who would have believed it?'

'Believed what?'

'Put on the telly. Mavis has surfaced and is giving press conferences. She says she is a victim.'

Agatha turned on the television and there indeed was Mavis. 'I have been the victim,' she was saying, 'of one publicity-seeking amateur detective. Agatha Raisin is not interested in finding out the identity of this murderer because she hasn't a clue. She is only interested in self-glorification. I am taking her to court.'

The phone started to ring. 'Don't answer it,' said Agatha.

One reporter suddenly stood up and said in a stentorian voice, 'Wait a minute. Agatha Raisin was savagely attacked and then buried under the church floor. Are you saying she did that herself?'

Agatha recognised a reporter from the *Sun* hustling Mavis away. The headlines in the *Sun* in the morning would be sympathetic to Mavis, but the other newspapers would not. The news presenter was saying, 'Of course, Agatha Raisin, who promised to reveal the identity of the murderer, did not. Sharon Elver, who went to school with Agatha Raisin, had this to say.' A dyed blonde with a middle-aged spread bulging over torn jeans said, 'Ooo! Our Aggie always was a bit of a liar. Boy mad she was. Always thinking up something to get attention so the fellows would notice her.'

'She wasn't even in my class,' wailed Agatha. 'What can I do, Toni, to stop this character assassination?'

Toni wanted to say, 'Stop telling lies about knowing who the murderer is.' Instead she said, 'Think! Why did

192

you think it was her anyway? What would prompt a lady of the village to murder, amongst others, her own twin?'

'Passion,' said Agatha. 'Blinding jealousy and passion. She is in love with the bishop.'

'Think of her as a chess piece. Get her to move,' urged Toni.

Agatha sat with her eyes half closed. A grandfather clock in the corner ticked away busily before giving an asthmatic cough and chiming seven strokes.

Suddenly, sitting up straight, Agatha reached for the phone. 'What are you going to do?' asked Toni.

Agatha phoned the *Mircester Telegraph* and asked for the following announcement to be added in time for the morning's issue. Toni listened uneasily as Agatha announced an engagement between herself and the bishop.

When Agatha had rung off, Toni said, 'The *Mircester Telegraph* will not only send a reporter here, they will inform the nationals as well. Couldn't you wait?'

'If I wait any longer for that bitch to ruin my reputation I won't have a client left. Let's go!'

'Agatha! You are not made of iron. You must still be weak, not to mention traumatised.'

'I've got it!' exclaimed Agatha. 'Do you remember that drugs case we solved for that posh nursing home? Let's see if they'll take me in. Nobody would think of looking for me there.'

'Well, that at least is sensible,' said Toni. 'And your case is still packed from the hospital. If only we could find that hammer.'

'The moment she surfaced, forensics – who had probably done a perfunctory test before – would take that manor house apart.'

A new French bakery had recently opened in Mircester, and so the bishop smiled down at the two delicious croissants on his breakfast plate the following morning.

He was just savouring the first mouthful when the dean crashed in and slammed the *Mircester Telegraph* down in front of him. 'What the hell are you up to now, Peter?'

'And what are you talking about to make your face go all red and puffy and your eyes bulge?'

'Oh, read the damn thing!' The dean stabbed one stubby finger down on the social column.

'It must be Agatha playing games,' said Peter after he had studied the announcement. 'She's trying to get my attention. She really fancies me.'

'Not one bit,' said the dean brutally. 'But what of all those other women you led to believe were soul mates? They'll be queueing up to ask you if it's true. Let's take that holiday.'

'First, I'd better phone the paper and put in a denial and then find Raisin and ask her what the hell she's playing at.'

'Get your secretary to do it.'

'She's busy writing a speech for me.'

Donald Whitby lit up a small cheroot, ignoring the

fact that the bishop was flapping the smoke away with exaggerated gestures.

'Mavis Dupin has been giving you a hard time,' he pointed out. 'If you let this announcement stand, and she comes yelling in here, tell her you are deeply in love with old bossy boots.'

'And what if old bossy boots, one Agatha Raisin, got it right and little Mavis is our murderer?'

'Rubbish. A tiny woman like that lifting up that gravestone and dumping Raisin underneath?'

'All right. But I am only doing it because she frightens me. I mean, bell ringing can give you muscles. And have you ever stopped to think about the real identity of the killer?'

'I think it was one of those bell ringers,' said the dean. 'Anyway, if she isn't around by this evening, we could clear off to Thailand tomorrow and by the time we get back, she'll be fantasising about someone else. I mean, you didn't have any physical contact with her, did you?'

'Of course not!!'

'Whisper naughty things in her ear?'

'You forget my position,' said Bishop Peter haughtily.

'I think you forgot it when you encouraged the droopy vicar's wife to tie up her husband.'

The bishop shrugged. 'I didn't tell her to clobber him one.'

The pair were sharing a bottle of fine old malt whisky. Only the dean knew that Peter was capable of savage outbursts of rage. But he asked as he had done a few times before, 'You have no idea where Jennifer Toynby is?'

The bishop smashed his fist on the table. 'Shut up! Just shut up!'

The bishop's secretary opened the door and ushered in Mavis Dupin. The bishop groaned inwardly. He had forgotten to tell her to admit no one. But he rose and drew out a chair for Mavis, remembering guiltily that he had managed to extract quite a bit of money from her.

Mavis held out the *Mircester Telegraph* with one trembling hand. 'Tell me this is not true.'

The dean waited for Peter to say it was indeed true but Peter said gently, 'How can it be true when you are the one I love?'

What's he playing at, wondered the dean.

'Please leave us, Donald,' said the bishop, who had just realised that if he could send Mavis away a happy woman then he could flee abroad the next morning.

When the dean had left the room, Peter said gently, 'I should have telephoned you. I have spoken to Mrs Raisin. She is crazy about me, poor woman. Ignore the paper.'

'I need proof of your commitment and loyalty to me,' said Mavis.

'I swear to you . . .'

'Actions speak louder than words. We are going to bed and I mean now.'

'But I have no . . . er . . . well . . . things to stop you getting pregnant.'

She flipped open a huge leather sack of a handbag. 'I have plenty.'

The door opened and the dean came in, adjusting his stole over a white cassock. 'Matins, my lord bishop.'

'Yes, yes, of course. Mavis, do you want to attend, or would you rather wait here?'

'I shall wait for you, my beloved.'

But when the service came to an end, Peter saw clearly a large number of the press waiting to speak to him.

In the vestry while they changed out of their robes, Donald whispered, 'I took the liberty of packing two bags and informing the canon to take over and that it was a family emergency.'

'Good man! What's the best way out? I can't think. She wants me to seduce her. She's sitting there in my study in all her dried-up, withered virginity clutching a hand-bag full of condoms. I wish you'd never thought up this old folks' home idea.'

'What? You were delighted. If I hadn't thought of it, you would have had to keep three elderly ladies in an expensive home.'

'Let me think.'

'The crypt!' exclaimed Donald. 'There's a little-used passage off where the choir boys keep their stuff. Thank goodness they weren't due at matins.'

They hurried off, finally reaching the car park. 'No press. We'll take your Ford. I keep expecting Mavis to come round the corner with a hammer.'

'So, you do think she murdered all those people?'

'No. Of course not. Get a move on!'

* * *

It began to dawn on Mavis that she had been dumped just like a sack of coal down an old coal-hole. At one point, the press had come knocking at the study door, but she had locked the door so that she and 'her lover' would not be disturbed as they exchanged their first passionate kisses. But when she realised the morning service was well and truly over, she unlocked the door and opened it. The bishop's secretary, Mary Frank, stood there.

'I was just about to get the spare key,' she said. 'His lordship has gone.'

'Gone? Where?'

'I don't know. He never tells me anything unless it's asking me to write another speech. Maybe he's gone to that fiancée of his.'

'He is not engaged to Agatha Raisin.'

'He didn't tell me to phone the *Telegraph* and tell them it was a mistake,' said Mary. 'Why don't you ask Mrs Raisin?'

'I shall do that,' said Mavis, stalking out, muttering, 'Remember you are a Dupin.'

James and Charles were at that moment glaring at Agatha. 'You mean,' shouted James, 'to sit here and hope she turns up to kill you with the weapon she used on the others? You are mad.'

'You're here to protect me,' said Agatha. 'I've let Toni go. Wouldn't want any harm to come to her.'

'Well, hear this,' said Charles. 'I have to remind you

again that I am not one of your employees. I am off on holiday and I suggest you phone your staff and get them over here.'

'Good idea,' said James. 'I'm off as well.'

'Look, I am sorry,' said Agatha. 'Can't you stay for a bit?'

To her dismay, neither answered. They simply walked out.

'Be like that!' Agatha yelled after them. 'A friend in need is a pain in the bum. Is that it?'

Silence.

That deep evening silence of the Cotswolds, which city-bred Agatha could never get quite used to, settled over the countryside.

Agatha phoned Patrick and he said he would round up the others and come over.

Now, out of the silence, Agatha began to hear the little whispers of the countryside. Things moved in the thatch. A dog barked. A car drove up to the end of Lilac Lane and stopped. Odd, thought Agatha, that there are no press ringing my bell. But I don't suppose our impending nuptials makes for great news.

Funnily enough, it would feel better if the murderer was the bishop rather than Mavis. Even though she must be out of her tiny gourd, she's a fellow sufferer tricked by love into insanity.

But is our bishop maybe not capable of another murder? I never did find out what happened to Jennifer Toynby. Then Ducksy went missing as well.

The doorbell rang, making her jump. She went to her

front door and looked through the spy hole. Patrick's lugubrious face looked back.

The welcoming smile faded from Agatha's face when she opened the door and heard Patrick say, 'She's got a gun in my back. Couldn't do anything else.'

'Inside. Both of you,' commanded Mavis.

Agatha's skull experienced a sharp pain as she remembered that vicious blow to the head.

Mavis ushered them into the kitchen. 'If anyone calls,' she said, 'you are to send them away. Got it?'

'Or you'll what?' demanded Agatha. 'Shoot me? You're going to do that anyway. So, you killed all these people and all because of a money-grabbing bishop.'

'Be quiet!' ordered Mavis.

The kitchen was brightly lit. Agatha studied Mavis. Then she thought of the murders.

The only thing that had made her worry about her judgement was that Millicent was so small – too small to dispose of bodies. Then she remembered Charles moaning about hosting the cricket club fête for his home, but saying he had to do it because some of the villagers were positively feudal and expected him to honour tradition.

'Oh, God!' she said. 'You didn't do it alone. You've got a helper.'

Mavis's eyes blazed for a moment. 'We will wait here until I am sure no one else is coming and then we will leave.'

James, thought Agatha frantically. You are only next door. Didn't you see her arrive?

But James had gone to see his wife to discuss divorce proceedings. Charles had reached home and was calling to Gustav to pack a suitcase.

Toni pulled up next to Mavis's car. 'I recognise that gas guzzler,' she said to Simon and Phil Marshall. 'It's that old Bentley from the manor house. Simon, call the police while I get round to Agatha's back garden and see if I can spot her. Phil, can you disable the car?'

'Easily.'

'Let's go.'

A calm had settled over Agatha. If I am going to die, she thought, I would like to know who helped Mavis. Let me think. Lady of the manor. Dupins there for ages. Someone who knows the church. Harry Bury, the sexton.

'It was Harry Bury,' said Agatha. 'You probably ordered him to. Poor bastard. But your own sister. How could you?'

'You don't know what it's like being a twin,' said Mavis. 'Same clothes and hairstyle while we were young. It was me that Peter invited to a party. She drugged my tea *and went as me.*

'She shouldn't have done that. I gave her a chance. I told her if she would swear on the Bible that she would never go near Peter again, I would forgive her. She laughed at me. Enough of this. On your feet and march.'

Patrick never took his eyes off the hand holding the gun.

If I come out of this alive, thought Agatha, I am going to get down on one knee and ask Charles to marry me.

Suddenly the whole scene was flooded with light and a stentorian voice called, 'You are surrounded. Put down that weapon and lie on the ground. You cannot escape.'

Patrick saw his moment. As Mavis raised the gun to Agatha's head, Patrick grabbed her wrist and broke it. When the gun fell to the ground, he kicked it away, brought out handcuffs, and handcuffed the crying, screaming Mavis.

Charles read about the arrest of Mavis in the English papers which he had bought that morning at a kiosk in Marseilles. His current girlfriend lay sprawled across the bed, snoring gently. She was blonde, curvaceous and quite stupid. Charles judged her to be in her early twenties. Agatha Raisin was middle-aged and intelligent. Forget her. This one was undemanding. On the other hand, Agatha Raisin would not get up during the night and empty most of his wallet. That could be considered demanding. Not that it made any difference because he had got up afterwards and taken it back along with some of her money.

They hadn't spoken much the night before. He had picked her up at a fish restaurant on the Corniche. She was English from somewhere in Essex and had boldly asked him if he would pay for her meal because she hadn't any money. He had agreed although he was sure she was lying. But she smiled a lot. And she wasn't Agatha.

He opened the *Daily Mail.* 'Oh, shiters!' yelled Charles. 'What's up?'

She was leaning up on one elbow. 'Tell you in a minute,' said Charles.

The arrest of Mavis Dupin had taken place too late in the day to get much show in anything but the stop press, but now the papers were having a field day.

''Ere! Chuck us one of them papers,' demanded the girl. 'Wot about breakfast?'

'Order something from room service ... er ... Holly,' he said, adding her name as he suddenly remembered it.

Holly ordered 'the full English' and then had to explain what she meant, settling at last for scrambled eggs and bacon and two rounds of toast along with a pot of coffee.

She picked up a copy of the *Sun* newspaper. 'Wot a bleedin' cow!' she exclaimed.

'What?'

'This detective woman. Says because she lured their chief reporter away from his wife and family, she got him killed. "I will never forgive him," said his wife. How did she do it? Nasty little eyes, she's got.'

'I've got to go back to England in a hurry,' said Charles. 'I'll pay the bill here so you can stay and finish your breakfast.'

'But you said you loved me!'

203

'I know I was drunk, but I have never in my life said I loved anybody.'

Charles began to throw his few clothes into a suitcase. He suddenly felt grubby and cheap. He shouldn't have left Agatha to cope. But she didn't need to cope on her own, yelled a voice inside his head. She had all her staff. Ignoring that voice, he left and paid the bill and ran all the way to the station.

Holly was furious to find that he had not only taken his own money back but some of hers as well. She was about to leave the room when she noticed the sun flickering on a pair of golf cuff links he had left behind. She weighed them in her hand and looked for the gold mark, having been trained in what to look for by her father who was currently doing time in Wormwood Scrubs. Eighteen carats. She had already noticed a pawn broker in one of the narrow lanes off the main boulevard. She found she was still hungry so she stopped in at a café and ordered two croissants with butter and jam and a hot chocolate. When the bill arrived, a man at the next table said, 'Let me get that for you.'

Her large blue eyes summed him up. English. Bit old. Not bad looking. Could always run away.

She batted her eyelashes. 'Now, that is sweet of you.'

And Charles, who had been known to brag that he never paid for sex, suddenly remembered those cuff links as the train pulled out of Marseilles. They had been a Christmas present from Agatha. All he needed to do was tell her he had lost them. She would never find out about Holly who was probably already clearing out the wallet of her next victim.

Agatha had told Bill Wong her suspicions that Harry Bury had been involved, not necessarily in committing the murders but by helping to try to hide the bodies. The police searched his cottage and work shed but found nothing incriminating. Harry, it seemed, was nothing more than a simple village man.

They would have changed their ideas if they could have heard a conversation he was having a week later with his crony, the butcher Joseph Merrydown.

'Won't it look a bit off, you clearing off to Bulgaria like that?' asked Joseph.

'Na! They ain't got nothing. You should come out and see the place. Tidy villa. Just outside Sofia.'

'Maybe. I'll lend you my passport in case they're watching the airports and you can post it back.'

'Okay.'

'But why did you help Mavis?'

'Why not? You should see the money in my account.'

'But there was no need to kill that reporter. The drinks he bought us!'

'I didn't kill him. It was that there Mavis. I didn't kill nobody. I done served her pa when he was alive. I've always served the Dupins and me father afore me.'

'What you got in Bulgaria?'

'I got a villa and a good-sized garden. Went on one of

those cheap package tours. The property was that cheap. Bought it for a rainy day. And now it's pouring. Can you take me to the Eurostar?'

'Sure, as long as you promise me a holiday.'

'Anytime.'

Agatha Raisin had never felt quite so low. Considering the morals of Fleet Street, she thought the reporters' attacks on *her* lack of morals disgraceful. From the days when she ran her own public relations company, she guessed that out of all the press she had entertained, only two had been faithful to their wives.

Mrs Bloxby called on her one Sunday evening. 'You haven't attended church for some time,' she said.

'I hardly ever go,' said Agatha. 'I am surprised you even noticed.'

'I thought you might be in need of help.'

'This is a bit embarrassing.'

'I would rather embarrass you, Mrs Raisin, than see you go under.'

'I am not going under!' shouted Agatha.

'Oh, really?' said the vicar's wife. 'Then why are your roots showing? And you have two brown hairs on your upper lip.'

'So,' sneered Agatha, 'you think I should go to church and ask God to dye my hair and shave my upper lip?'

'Well, why not?'

The friends glared at each other and then Mrs Bloxby began to giggle. Agatha took a mirror out of her handbag. 'Oh, dear. I have let myself go. My reputation is lower than whale poo. Have a sherry. I'll have one as well. Okay, I will get to the beautician and hairdresser tomorrow. I thought Charles would be around but Jerry Cranton over in Shipston said he was in Marseilles one evening and Charles was squiring a blonde totty. You know, I had planned to ask Charles to marry me. How odd. He's only a few years younger and yet I forget all men like them far younger.' A tear rolled down Agatha's cheek.

'You need to get away,' urged the vicar's wife. 'Pack up and go for a holiday. I know. Phuket.'

'And so say all of us,' said Agatha.

'No, I wasn't swearing. Phuket in Thailand. Sun and sea. You need to get away from it all.'

'I will think about it.'

The more Agatha thought about taking a holiday, the better the idea seemed. She booked two weeks in Phuket and, while there, felt the tension leave her body for the first time in weeks. Her hair was glossy again and misery had made her lose pounds. At the end of her stay, she was idly listening to two men talking at the next table. It was hard not to listen because they had such loud, braying voices.

'We went out for dinner and she said it was a good restaurant but there was this awful smell of decaying fish. But she led me on and when I went in for the kill, she pushes me away and says she has found God.'

'That's a new line in rejection,' said his friend.

Agatha leaned towards them. 'I couldn't help over-hearing you. Was the lady's name Ducksy?'

'Yes, it was as a matter of fact. Turned out she and her pal live in some sort of commune. There's a leaflet about it at the hotel desk.'

Agatha picked up a leaflet at the reception desk. It was an advertisement for All God's Children at eye-watering prices for what it claimed was a road back to the simple life. Agatha called a cab and set out.

It was nearly thirty kilometres away. The commune appeared to consist of thatched cottages, built round a small lake. Among the cottages was a church and from the church came the sound of voices raised in hymns.

Agatha sat on a bench outside the church and waited for the service to end. When they started to stream out, Agatha hailed Ducksy. 'Do you know, everyone back home has been looking for you? Is Jennifer Toynby here as well?'

'Yes, poor lamb. She was so pixilated with the bishop, hoping to get her hands under the purple, but all he wanted was her money. Same with me. He and that dean can be terrifying.'

'Are they an item?'

'No. I saw them last week. They were here on holiday. They like very young girls. I mean *very* young. Jennifer! Over here.'

After the introductions had been made, Agatha said, 'People thought the bishop had bumped you off.'

'I know, I wanted him to sweat. Money-grabbing

rotter. Have you come to join us? God can help with everything.'

'So I've heard,' said Agatha, thinking of Mrs Bloxby and beginning to laugh. Then she said, 'Did he help with new passports?'

'Actually, our reverend said if I really wanted to disappear, I should claim to have lost my passport and get a new one and hide out until then. Easy-peasy.'

Agatha looked at them curiously. 'But surely you've left one lot trying to get your money and landed on another.'

'But Reverend Sam is genuine. He sees the future. Oh, do go away. You have an unclean spirit.'

A week later, Joseph Merrydown arrived in Bulgaria for a holiday with Harry Bury.

'Is this it?' complained Joseph. 'I mean, it's freezing. I thought it would be beaches and sunshine.'

'Wrong country,' said Harry. 'Come in and see the place. Have a drink.'

'This ain't half bad,' said Joseph, looking round a cosy living room with a big log fire. 'I envy you and that's a fact. I suppose I can stay as long as I like, hey? You wouldn't want me blabbing, now, would you?'

'I hope that was a joke. Here, have some of the local brandy.'

Joseph sat in an armchair by the fire, sipping the brandy and wishing he could stay forever. He was only a retired butcher. His wife had died ten years before without leaving him any children. He would give it a week and see how he and Harry got on. Should be all right. They had been friends for years. Lulled by the brandy and the fire, he drifted off to sleep. Harry watched him and fretted. He felt sure he would have a hard time getting rid of him. Had he told anyone where he was going? Harry was sure he had not because he had promised never to tell anyone at all where he, Harry, had gone.

But it was a risk. He knew that Mavis had not told anyone about his part in the murders or the Bulgarian police would have picked him up by now. Joseph and he looked a bit alike, both having red faces and squat, powerful bodies. If Joseph died, I could take his identity, he thought. Then I could take trips back home. I like it here but I miss England. Yes, that would do it. But I couldn't go back to Thirk Magna as Joseph. All those ringers would notice the difference like a shot.

He went out to the garage where he found a bottle of antifreeze. He poured a good measure of it into the decanter which held the local brandy. He knew of old that Joseph liked his drink. He was about to carry the decanter back to the living room when he wondered what he would do about the farm tenancy. He stopped in the kitchen, hit by a sudden thought. Would he be expected to wind it up in person? Or would a letter do? He'd need to forge Joseph's signature. Leave it till later, he decided. He put the decanter with the mixture of brandy and antifreeze in a cupboard, opened another squat bottle, filled another decanter and carried it into the living room where he found Joseph awake.

'I wish I hadn't come by train,' said Joseph. 'Right tiring, it is.'

'Farm as hard work as ever?'

'No. Turned over the tenancy. Got one of them little alms-houses down by the pub. Not much room, mind, but it suits me. Don't you worry that Mavis might blab?'

'Not her. Bonkers. Said she's not fit to stand trial.'

'Didn't the authorities get curious when you started moving your money to Bulgaria?'

'Took it all out in cash. Started hiding it from the day old man Dupin started paying me to cover up.'

'Cover up, like what?'

'Like when he got that simple kid, Florrie, pregnant. I was the one who paid the family to shut up and get an abortion. Dirty old bastard he was. Think his wife died o' disgust. So Mavis knew where to go for help. Terrified o' prison. Thousands she paid me.'

'Come through to the kitchen. Got a bit o' stew for dinner.'

The stew was delicious. 'Never knew you could cook like this, Harry,' said Joseph.

'I can't. There's a woman down the village who does takeaway meals.'

Joseph wanted another drink but Harry had only served water with the meal. As Harry put things away in cupboards, Joseph saw that decanter of brandy.

* * *

Later that night, Joseph lay awake, listening to the wind and longing for a drink. It had strangely enough not seemed all that bad back in England when Harry had first confessed to helping Mavis. But here in this foreign country, it felt sinister and dangerous.

He remembered that decanter. Just one drink.

Harry awoke in the morning, opened the shutters and found snow had been falling all night. His thoughts of the previous evening of killing Joseph and taking his identity seemed madness. He opened the cupboard to get that decanter out and empty the contents down the sink, and saw, to his alarm, that it wasn't there anymore.

Swearing under his breath, he went into the living room. Joseph was lying back in the armchair, his face an odd pinkish-purple colour. The decanter was empty. He had doctored another decanter just in case but it was still in the kitchen cupboard.

Harry sat down suddenly. If he reported Joseph dead, the British embassy in Sofia would investigate as well as the local police. It was doubtful if they would come to the right conclusion because Harry had watched enough crime documentaries to learn that they do not usually hit on the right answer. But he could get rid of Joseph's body and claim he had left – that was if anyone was curious enough to ask or even knew he had arrived in Bulgaria.

There was an old well in the courtyard. Harry rose stiffly and went out of doors. He heaved the thick teak covering from the top of the well. He threw a stone down. It was a long time until he heard a splash. He took a wheelbarrow through to the living room and loaded Joseph's stiffening body onto it, wheeled the body back to the well and tipped it in.

That's that, he thought. I'll stay on here as me and travel as old Joseph, use his passport, and stop worrying that Mavis has recovered her wits enough to blab.

But he felt suddenly lonely and, for the first time, longed to go home again and never leave.

Agatha had never been without Charles's company for so long. She missed him, but the scandal about her affair with Terry and his subsequent murder had died away and she was busy with the usual bread-and-butter round of divorces, missing people and animals and industrial espionage. James was always travelling. His divorce was due any day now.

Toni came to Agatha's desk one morning and said, 'Read that little paragraph.'

Agatha read, '"British home owner found dead with another Britisher in a Bulgarian village, Saint Gregory. Cause of death appeared to come from a dead body found down a well which supplied the water to the house. The dead are identified as Harry Bury and Joseph Merrydown, both from the Cotswold village of Thirk Magna." Remember them? Two of the bell ringers.'

'Yes, I do. You would think a countryman would know where his water supply came from,' said Agatha.

'And what were they doing in Bulgaria? I am going over to Thirk Magna to find out.'

'You know,' said Toni, 'the Cotswolds are so well run and so picturesque that people have got used to all the same amenities they have in the cities. Harry probably thought his water came off the mains.'

'The body down the well is interesting. It really does look as if Mavis may not have bumped them all off.' Agatha hesitated in the doorway. 'Anyone heard from Charles?'

'Not a word,' said Toni.

Agatha found out from Helen Toms who said, 'Harry Bury had finished his farm tenancy and disappeared one day and after getting an alms house, too! Then his best friend, Joseph Merrydown, left, saying he was going on holiday but not where, and for the first time we don't have enough bell ringers.'

All in that moment, Agatha decided she must go to Bulgaria. How awful it would be if Mavis was not the only murderer.

'Why bother?' asked Toni. 'Leave it to the police.'

But Agatha felt that if she could prove something that the police had missed, she might be able to restore some of the pride she once had in her detective abilities.

Toni was sitting at Agatha's desk three days later, looking through the files of jobs still to be done. Patrick and Phil accepted the fact that Agatha always put the young girl in charge, but Simon was apt to get mutinous about it and slack off.

She had closed up for the day and scowled when she heard someone coming up the stairs. A voice called, 'Hi! It's Charles. I'm back!'

Toni unlocked the door. 'She's not here. Gone to Bulgaria.'

'Why?'

'Loose ends in the Mavis case.'

'Oh, the stupid woman. Mavis is locked up in a psychiatric prison. So, what now? I'll buy you dinner and you can tell me all about it.'

'Can't risk it,' said Toni. 'I am saving up for a new flat.'

'What on earth is that supposed to mean?'

'It means we'll go to an expensive restaurant and you will as usual have forgotten your wallet, so come in and sit down and listen.'

Charles half turned to go because he thought a young girl like Toni should show more respect and . . . oh, he'd better find out about Agatha.

'To make it short,' began Toni. She succinctly outlined the little she knew.

Charles groaned. 'If there is any truth behind her suspicions, maybe someone else will crop up in her fevered brain.'

'Do you miss her?' asked Toni.

'Of course. We are friends. There are plenty of women around for the other thing.'

Toni sighed and switched on the computer. 'Like mindless sex?'

Charles looked at the glowing blonde beauty that was Toni and his eyes sharpened.

Without taking her eyes off the computer screen, Toni said, 'Don't even think about it.'

'Wasn't,' lied Charles, but thinking that Toni was showing all the mind-reading intuition that her boss had on a good day.

He decided to drive over to Thirk Magna. He was just in time for Evensong. The vicar was showing no signs of being battered. In fact, he looked smugger than ever. But he did have a beautiful voice as he read the third collect. '"Lighten our darkness, we beseech thee, O Lord; and by thy great mercy defend us from all perils and dangers of this night; for the love of thine only Son, our Saviour, Jesus Christ: Amen."'

Charles suddenly realised sharply how much he missed Agatha. Only Agatha would understand that somehow when you stood in one of these ancient churches, the old sinister medieval Cotswolds that believed in witches seemed to seep out of the very stones.

He had run away from the temptation of asking her to marry him. And all because the county would think her out of place: opening the annual fête, making speeches, playing croquet, all those things his aunt coped with in her creaky way. And Gustav would leave him.

But what if she married someone else? It suddenly didn't bear thinking of. Even now, a lonely Agatha out in some godforsaken Bulgarian village might be promising to marry some dandruffed wanker while he sat in this creepy church singing, 'Abide with Me.'

Epilogue

Agatha was sitting in a Stalinist-type hotel wondering what on earth had possessed her to come. She had wanted proof that Joseph had been poisoned. The police inspector had been firm but polite in his dismissal. Then came a visit from the British consul telling her to go home.

Harry had made a will in which he had left everything to his only surviving relative, a cousin from Birmingham called Sarah Jinks, a spinster lady of quite terrifying gentility. She had arrived the day before but turned a deaf ear to Agatha's pleading to have a look in the house.

Agatha, in order to keep her trim figure, had ordered a salad for her starter. It came with great square white blocks of what looked like feta cheese on top. Chewing the first one, she found it was lard and had to spit it out into her napkin. The piped music was recordings of Russian fishermen's songs which all seemed to end each chorus with a yell of 'Hi!'

She had ordered the set meal, the next course being ravioli. But it turned out to be ravioli stuffed with bear, which she thought she could refuse on the grounds that it was fattening, but then spoiled it all by ordering cherry cake with double cream and a glass of slivovitz.

The food in the villages was reported to be very good but hitherto she had felt too put down at her lack of success to feel like eating anything when she was there.

She pulled out her mobile phone to call the airline and see if she could change her ticket when Charles sat down opposite her.

Agatha smiled. Charles blinked. He had forgotten that smile of Agatha's that, when she was happy, could light up a whole room.

'Oh, Charles, where have you been?'

'Marking time, I think,' he said. 'I gather you hope to find that Harry was the second murderer.'

'It stands to reason. You don't chuck your pal down a well unless you've knocked him off. But there's a Miss Gentility got the villa now and she won't let me in. Oh, Charles! You've got a title. If only you were a lord and not just a sir.'

'Sorry. Great-grandad didn't pay Lloyd George enough.'

'Come with me tomorrow.'

'I might have an excuse to get us in there.'

'Like what?'

'I went to Evensong at Thirk Magna, and Gloria the bell-ringing blonde tells me that Harry tried to pay her to go to bed with him and said he kept all the stuff in the house and didn't fancy banks. Let her think we know where the stuff might be and I'll bet she lets us in. What's the food like?'

'Ghastly.'

Charles called the waiter over and asked for chocolate cake and a glass of slivovitz and ordered him to turn the music down.

'How did you do that?' marvelled Agatha. 'They wouldn't do it for me.'

'This is a man's country. Home of the chauvinist pig. I might move here.'

'And I want to hear about your travels.'

'Let's take the cake and brandy upstairs. I'm in your room.'

'You can't do that!'

'It's a double room.'

'Then keep to your bed and get up early to go with me to the villa.'

'Yes, ma'am.'

Not yet, thought Agatha sleepily. Tomorrow, we'll sleep together after I have proposed.

Why don't we just get married? thought Charles. Agatha is never boring.

The countryside was covered in snow as they made their way to Harry's villa. The car Agatha had rented did not feel very secure, having rather worn-out tyres.

Sarah Jinks answered the door and scowled horribly

when she saw Agatha. 'I told you to get lost,' she said, the refinement gone from her voice and the Brummie accent peeping through.

Charles stepped forward. He had dressed with care and looked his best. 'Haven't we met before?' he asked. 'My card.'

She glanced at his card and then looked closer and her face went through a series of odd convulsions, settling on what she might have thought a winning smile.

'I have been to a fête at your house, Sir Charles. What a coincidence! And here is little me and you in the wilds of nowheah. I am surprised you should be with a private detective.'

'Mrs Raisin is an old friend, the Berkshire Raisins, you know.'

'Oh, Mrs Raisin, you should have said something. I usually recognise quality but I was thet flustered with all these foreign folks. Do come in. Come in. The kitchen is warm. I have coffee ready. Why don't we have a cup and maybe a leetle shot of the local brandy?'

'That would be very kind,' said Charles.

Sarah Jinks had stubby lashes which she batted at Charles. 'Are you two an item?'

'Yes,' said Agatha.

'No,' said Charles.

Sarah waggled a finger under Agatha's nose. 'I know where you are at, my dear. We do keep hoping.'

Agatha let out a yelp of pain for Charles had kicked her under the table to suppress the quite horrible remark he saw rising to Agatha's lips.

'Arthritis, dear?' asked Sarah. 'An elderly aunt of mine has it something crool.'

'I would just *love* some brandy,' said Charles loudly.

When Sarah got up and went to open one of the kitchen cupboards, Charles whispered, 'We want to search this place, get it? So shut up.'

Sarah began to pour slivovitz into tiny glasses.

'What is the toast in Bulgarian?' asked Sarah.

'Up yours, I think,' muttered Agatha, and then yelped as Charles knocked her glass from her hand.

'It's the sweet taste, Agatha,' said Charles. 'Sarah, don't drink it. It has antifreeze in it. That must be how Joseph was killed.'

'I will call the police,' shrieked Sarah.

'Before you do that,' said Charles, 'did you know that Harry hid a fortune in banknotes in this house? If you phone the police right away, they will turn the place over thoroughly and if they find any money, you will have years of bureaucratic trouble getting it.'

'You look. Go on,' she said in her normal voice. 'This is all too much.'

Agatha and Charles searched all day. There was a safe in a dusty office but it contained nothing but old farm records. Finally, they told Sarah to call the police but not to mention the money.

'And I thought Wilkes back in Mircester was bad,' moaned Agatha as they got back to the hotel at midnight. 'Questions and more questions and hand over our passports. And I am so hungry.'

'Relax. I have with me in this large canvas bag a beef casserole from the takeaway café in the village. I got it when I was out filling up the petrol tank. This elderly gentleman who is leering and bowing and scraping will let us use the kitchens. Do grease his palm with something, Aggie, and stop glaring at me.'

Agatha thought she was giving the old waiter a ten euro note but actually it was a fifty euro note.

She snatched her hand away as he looked as if he wanted to kiss it all night.

Seated in the kitchen with the casserole heated and served and a reasonable bottle of wine on the table, Agatha said, 'I have a sudden idea.'

'Like what?'

'I doubt if Sarah has any money of her own. Now, if a pair of people landed on my doorstep and told me that there was possibly a fortune in banknotes in the house, I would join in the search. But she didn't. You know why?'

'Tell me, Sherlock.'

'Because she's found it already. So, should it be true, do we tell the police?'

'No, let her have it. You've made your point, Aggie. She's invited us for lunch tomorrow. We'll call round at police headquarters and see if we can leave.' He scowled out at the falling snow. 'Agatha, I don't usually have flashes of intuition like you, but I have a creepy feeling that we are going to be stuck here for days, even weeks.'

'That's just depression. It's a poor place and it's cold and we are far from home. Let's go.'

They returned to the casserole dish, and bought another casserole, of lamb this time for the evening, and were crawling through a blinding blizzard when Charles skidded to a halt.

'Don't tell me we have to walk,' moaned Agatha. 'These boots are definitely not made for walking.'

'That's because they've got stupid high heels. Another ten years and you will have bunions.'

'Did you stop to give me a lecture on my footwear?'

'I was wondering if murdering tendencies run in families. She may ask us when we arrive if we told the police about the money. If we say "no", she may kill us. Maybe she's been up all night thinking if she got rid of us, she and the money would be safe.'

Charles started the car again and crawled on, stopping at last in front of the hotel with a grunt of relief. 'Amazing the way this old banger makes it, but unless the snow ploughs come out tonight, we won't be seeing Jinks tomorrow.'

'Let's make notes,' said Agatha, after dinner. 'Where would you hide banknotes? He doesn't have a library. Just a couple of paperbacks. Somewhere dry.'

'I gather he bought the house which was being sold separate from the land,' said Charles. 'There is a shed, a garage and a couple of broken-down outbuildings. Nothing very weatherproof. Why are you scowling?'

'I cannot remember Mavis actually confessing to the murders.'

'Last report was that she was mad and probably unfit to stand trial, but for the police the fact that she came after you with a gun was enough and she must have stated something before she went round the bend.'

'I am so tired,' said Agatha. 'Let's go to bed.'

'I'll finish this wine. You go ahead.'

By the time Charles got upstairs it was to find Agatha fast asleep. He wondered whether to climb into bed beside her, but she had left her bedside lamp on and he saw the mark of tears on her cheeks. What had made her cry?

But when he asked her over breakfast, she shrugged and said she must have been having a bad dream. Agatha would not of course tell him that she no longer had the courage to propose to him. She guessed she was faced with the prospect of a lonely old age.

'The snowplough has been out,' said Agatha. 'Do you really think she might bump us off?'

'Maybe.'

'How?'

'Dunno. Smack on the back of the head with a shovel. Rat poison in the coffee. Or, here's a thought, the one place we did not search was her bedroom because it seemed then an intrusion and she had locked the door.'

'That must be it. How do we get in there?'

'If we could drug her . . . hang on, I see the old retainer

who you must have tipped a fortune because he is smiling and nodding and leering. Leave him to me.'

When Charles came back, he said, 'Now we wait.'

'What for?'

'His nephew is a pharmacist. I asked for a really powerful sleeping pill. We'll drug her coffee.'

'You know, Charles,' said Agatha, 'if we find the money, I don't want to give it to her. Now, if we told the police and indicated we would keep silent about it *if* we had our passports back, they might be obliging.'

'They'd charge us with bribery.'

'Not if we are very subtle. I, Charles, am always very subtle.'

'As a sledgehammer. Don't pout.'

Agatha sat in grim silence until the servant came back with the sleeping pills. Together they got into the rented car.

'Don't sulk,' said Charles eventually.

'I am not sulking.'

'Suit yourself, sweetie. But this car is fogging up with sulk.'

'Oh, all right,' said Agatha. 'But I don't like put-downs. Anyway, this might be like the prisoners' get-together. She tries to poison us while we try to drug her.'

'Play it by ear. Tell her we've come to say good-bye. When she knows we are no longer a threat, you can slip the drug into her coffee.'

226

'No, you do it. She'll be so busy fawning over you, she won't notice.'

Sarah Jinks welcomed them with a false enthusiasm which became genuine when they told her they were leaving. 'So sorry to lose you. That jug of coffee is a leetle old.' She poured it down the sink. 'It'll only take a moment to make a new one.'

I wonder if that old one had the poison in, thought Agatha. Now that she thinks we are leaving, she feels she has nothing to fear.

When cups of coffee had been poured all round, Agatha said, 'May I use your toilet? I hope it's not out in the yard.'

'No, no. Let me show you.'

The moment they had both left, Charles put a large slug of sleeping draught into Sarah's coffee.

When they came back, Sarah obviously having waited until Agatha had finished in case she walked off somewhere, she fluttered about, offering biscuits, sugar and milk. At last, she drank a large gulp of coffee. 'This is stuff I brought from dear old Blighty,' she said. 'The local brew is horrible. I think they make it out of ...' She suddenly slumped forward and Charles caught her head before it banged against the table.

'Give me that cushion and I'll make her comfortable.'

'I hope you haven't killed her,' said Agatha.

'Don't suppose so. Let's get on with it. Look for keys. Her handbag is on the dresser.'

Agatha rummaged in the handbag and brought out a ring of keys. 'Let's try her room.'

227

They unlocked her bedroom door. It was a sparsely furnished room. A wardrobe held a few coats; a chest of drawers with nothing but underwear and socks and sweaters. The bedside table had only one thing in it: a Gideon Bible.

'I am beginning to feel we've been making a terrible mistake and if that woman does not realise we drugged her then she is stupider than she seems,' said Agatha, ripping back the bedclothes. 'Oh, how sweet. Her bedtime reading, *Lady Veronica's Fancy*. Pah!'

'We may as well give up,' said Charles, 'and later, I will romance her and claim she had a seizure.'

'She will probably fall for it, thinking she's Lady Veronica. Wait a moment. My eyes just fell on the blurb. It says that Veronica was being forced into marriage with an evil old man and as she had no money of her own, she could not escape. But the ghost of her mother appeared and told her to look in the chimney and there she found . . .'

'The family jewels!' cried Charles.

They collided on the hearth in their excitement. Charles thrust his arm up the chimney. 'Got something.' He pulled and a canvas bag came tumbling down.

He opened it. It was stuffed to the top with Bank of England notes.

'We've got her,' said Agatha. 'I know, you phone the police. I will hide behind the curtains. If they just count out the notes and write down the amount, we are stuck. But if they start to share some of it, we've got our passports back.'

'Okay. But be careful. If it's that inspector, he's pretty sharp.'

Two rather slovenly policemen arrived. One seemed to speak good English, explaining that he had relatives in Manchester. Agatha watched them enter the room. Then they turned to Charles and told him to wait downstairs. They crouched over the bag, speaking rapidly in Bulgarian. Agatha taped every word. Then they counted out wads of notes and hid them in their pockets before counting out what, Agatha gathered, would be officially declared. She taped their conversation, wishing they would hurry up, because she was beginning to feel cramped.

At last what sounded like a higher official came into the room and barked orders. Agatha sighed with relief when they had all left.

The higher official that Agatha thought she'd heard was in fact the chief inspector, who was at that moment in the kitchen, questioning Charles about finding the money and demanding that a doctor examine Sarah.

'I searched her handbag for drugs and found these,' said Charles, handing over the bottle of sleeping draught. 'People do get addicted to these things.'

Agatha entered the room. 'Where have you been?' demanded the inspector.

'In the lavatory.'

'You will both need to be searched to make sure you have not taken any of the money.'

'Before you do that,' said Agatha, 'I want you to listen to this and I want you to agree that the quicker you return our passports and get us back home, the better for you.'

She took out her powerful little tape recorder and switched it on.

'That's enough!' shouted the inspector. 'Give me that.'

'Passports first.'

He grabbed Agatha's wrist and gave it a painful twist. The recorder went flying up in the air. Charles seized it and fled out of the house and they could hear him driving off a few minutes later.

Agatha was wondering whether crying would relieve the rage and misery she felt as she sat in a smelly village police station. She was shivering with cold and very hungry. Was she always going to go mad when she thought of any man? Marry Charles? That faithless man was probably back in Britain by now.

She had shouted for the British consul, for a lawyer, for anyone to help, but there was only a desk sergeant left to guard her and he appeared deaf to her every request.

She had fallen into a shivering sleep when the cell door was opened and there was Charles, shaking her awake and shouting, 'Get a move on! I've got our passports.'

* * *

They parted at dawn at Heathrow Airport and went to get their respective cars. Charles had explained the delay in getting her freedom by saying he had gone to the main newspaper offices. From there, he had phoned the police. Meetings had gone on for ages, until it was agreed the newspaper would only do a story about the money being found but nothing about the police theft of some of it. The passports were handed over but he was told firmly that no money had been taken by the police. Charles kept Agatha's tape recorder as insurance that they would be allowed the leave the country. Sarah Jinks swore she did not know anything about any money and as there was no proof to contradict this, she was not charged.

'Charles!' called Agatha to his retreating back.

He slowly walked back towards her, but his face had the shuttered look he put on when he did not want to hear anything at all.

'Hurry up, Aggie,' he said. 'I just want to get home.'

'Nothing,' said Agatha sadly.

As he walked away from her again, she turned to lift her two heavy suitcases off the luggage trolley because she always believed in travelling as heavy as possible.

'Let me help you with that,' said a male voice. Agatha swung round. A tall man stood there, smiling down at her. She had a quick impression of an attractive face and thick brown hair.

She suddenly smiled that radiant smile of hers, a smile that Charles saw as he began to drive off.

He stopped beside them. 'See you soon!' he called.

'Who was that?' asked Agatha's new friend.

'Just some chap who works for me. I'm a detective,' said Agatha.

'I would love to hear about your work. Dinner sometime? Here is my card.'

Inspector Wilkes received statements from the police in Sofia along with a signed confession written by Harry Bury as to his help in the murders which Sarah had found and had concealed up in the rafters. It nailed the responsibility for all the murders squarely on Mavis Dupin's thin shoulders.

'It's that Raisin woman,' Wilkes grumbled to Bill Wong. 'There's also a long report from her about finding those women in Phuket.'

'Considering how she was pilloried in the newspapers about her affair with that reporter, it might be a nice gesture to give her credit for something. She is a good detective.'

'Wash your mouth out with soap. She's an interfering busybody who got lucky.'

Two weeks later, Charles thought he should rouse himself and go and see Agatha. But there had been so much work to be done on the estate, so much to catch up on. Also, he had sensed uneasily that Agatha was beginning to look on him as a prospective husband.

But that must have been his imagination because she

had not tried to get in touch with him, forgetting that when she did, Gustav often blocked the calls.

It was a fine, late-spring evening when he set out. How dreary the Cotswolds were in winter, he thought, and how staggeringly beautiful in the spring when all the blossoms came out.

To his surprise, Lilac Lane, where Agatha lived, was blocked with parked cars. He could see lights streaming out from all the windows of Agatha's thatched cottage. A gentle voice behind him said, 'Going to the party, Sir Charles?'

'Mrs Bloxby! Agatha didn't invite me.'

'Perhaps your man forgot to give it to you. We must hope she will be happy this time.'

'This time what?'

Mrs Bloxby suddenly wished herself elsewhere. 'Marriage. It is her engagement party to some man she met at the airport only a few weeks ago.'

'You go ahead, Mrs Bloxby. I'll follow you.'

He stood under the sweet blossoms of the lilac trees for about ten minutes and then he went slowly forwards. He stood outside the sitting room. Agatha was standing next to that man he had seen her with in the car park. He began to back away although she surely could not see him in the darkness.

But the streetlamp above his head came on and Agatha looked straight at him. All the memories of all the times they had had together flashed through Charles's mind. He turned away slowly and walked off into the night.

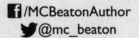